ELIZA PROKOPOVITS

Ember and Twine

Contents

Ember and Twine

Ember skidded to a stop outside the back door of the cottage. Mamma's and Miss Tearsha's raised voices rang out from the kitchen. Ember didn't want to meet Miss Tearsha today. She leaned against the door, listening, even though she knew it was rude.

"He was my *husband!*"

"Yes, and thank you for rubbing it in." Miss Tearsha's voice, always silky smooth, was icy. "But, you see, *Twine*," she said, using Mamma's name like a curse word, "his death already makes the villagers nervous. *You* already make the villagers nervous. So it's better all around if you're not there."

There was a frigid pause. Ember pictured ice crystals forming around the windows. Finally, Mamma spoke.

"We will leave in the morning."

"You'll do no such thing, *witch*," Miss Tearsha hissed. "You could kill us all by then."

Ember forgot that she was pretending to not be there. She was so angry that she burst through the door, interrupting the tense scene in the tiny kitchen. Before she could say a word, however, Mamma grabbed her and hugged her close, pressing Ember's face into her shoulder so that she couldn't mouth off to their unwelcome guest.

"You'll leave immediately," Miss Tearsha said, a hint of triumph in her cold voice. She turned and stalked out of the house.

Mamma waited until the door slammed behind her. She released Ember. "You hid them?"

Ember nodded.

"Good. Get your cloak. Say goodbye to your Da. It's time to go."

Ember ran to get her cloak from the hook by the front door. It was green and thick and warm, really too warm for the late summer, but it would get cold outside at night. Ember bundled it in her arms and hugged it, then paced slowly toward the single bedroom. Da lay on the bed, unmoving. He had died in the night from an unexplained fever. The healers hadn't been able to do anything for him, though they'd tried. Da was well loved in the village. The villagers would bury him tomorrow. Ember and Mamma wouldn't be there.

Ember hesitated in the doorway but couldn't think of anything to say. At last she walked over and kissed Da's cold cheek, just like she used to do in the evening when he came in from cutting wood in the forest. Tears welled in her eyes, and she fled to the kitchen where Mamma was waiting. Mamma nodded and led the way out of the house, through the front door so that Miss Tearsha and anyone else watching could see that they were really leaving. They didn't lock up; it wasn't their house anymore.

Mamma held Ember's hand as they walked the length of the village to the gate. Ember had been known to vault the fence that protected the village at a spot much closer to the cottage, but Mamma would never, and this wasn't the time. Ember felt eyes watching her from doorways and windows, but she tried not to look at them. She couldn't help glancing at a couple of houses to see if her friends were watching. Sean gave a small wave before disappearing behind the curtain.

The fence was a beautiful, if odd looking, barrier between the village and the outside world. It was only about as high as Ember's waist, and it was made of a combination of wood and twine. Ember always thought the fence was too short to actually be a defense. But travelers had brought stories of werewolves and vampires and all kinds of terrible things from the surrounding woods, and some of them had been pretty convincing. No awful creatures had ever come into the village, though, so maybe the fence *did* work.

Mamma opened the gate and closed it carefully behind them. She took Ember's hand again, and they continued along the path away from the village into the first trees of the forest until the dark afternoon shadows closed in behind them. Mamma stopped and turned to Ember.

"Where did you hide them?"

"Just up here." Ember pointed. She towed Mamma a little farther along the path and then off into the woods to the right. She stopped at the foot of the tree she'd chosen. Mamma squinted up. She raised a hand to touch Ember's hairband then nodded. Ember passed her the cloak she was still hugging and started climbing.

Mamma made all of Ember's clothing—most mothers in the village did—and she made sure that they had lots of pockets and were good for climbing. But there were a few items that she was particular about. The hairband was one of them. Ember's hair never stayed neatly in its braid, so Mamma had made her the hairband to keep it out of her face. The band was blue, and Ember had watched Mamma make it with a hook and thread.

Most mothers in the village could do it; even some of the girls Ember's age. Mamma always said there would be plenty of time for Ember to learn later, and since she'd rather be running outdoors and climbing trees, she didn't argue. But Mamma always made sure that she had the hairband on when she went out, and that it was still there when she came home.

Ember had chosen this tree not only because it was an easy climb but also because there was a hollow a little way up that was perfect for hiding things. It couldn't be seen from below. She pulled out the bags she had stashed less than an hour before. Mamma had filled one of the bags when Da had first gotten sick. When Ember had asked, she said that it was just a precaution. When Da had gotten worse, Mamma had begun packing the others; she hadn't slept last night as she gathered everything she thought they'd need. Ember had lain awake in the little made-up bed in the kitchen, listening to Mamma muttering to herself. She'd bitten her lip against the sad and terrified tears that threatened to spill over. When Mamma had piled the last of the bags by the back door and gone into the other room, she'd let the tears come, crying herself to sleep. She woke only a couple of hours later with a headache and gritty, puffy eyes.

Ember dropped the bags to Mamma then swung back down and landed with a thump. There were five bags. Three of them were very light. Mamma slung two of these across Ember's back before handing her back her cloak, then shouldered the other three herself.

Ember looked over her shoulder at one of the bags she was carrying. "What's in these?"

"Yarn." At Ember's raised eyebrows, Mamma said, "We'll need it all and more, believe me. Let's go—we need to get as far as we can before sundown."

Ember glanced around at the deepening shadows. Even in late summer, sundown wasn't far away.

They returned to the path and hurried on. Mamma seemed distracted. Ember twice had to tug on her hand to keep her from tripping over a fallen branch that jutted too far into the path. Once she muttered aloud, "They'll regret it once the fence fails."

"What, Mamma?" Ember asked.

"Nothing," Mamma said.

After a moment, Ember said, "Mamma, why did Miss Tearsha call you a witch?"

"She was just being unkind."

"Are you angry?" Angry would explain why she was so distracted.

"Not about that."

Ember led Mamma around a low-hanging branch that she was too distracted to avoid. "What are you angry about?"

"I'm angry that they wouldn't let us stay to bury Da," Mamma said softly, squeezing Ember's hand. "And I'm angry that the rest of the village is foolish enough to listen to Tearsha. They ought to know better after all our family has done in the village."

Ember thought she knew what Mamma meant. Da's family had lived in the village forever, and so had Mamma's. Everyone spoke of Ember's great-grandmamma with respect bordering on awe, even though no one ever bothered to tell Ember much about her. Ember did know, though, that when they were young, Miss Tearsha had wanted to marry Da but he'd chosen Mamma instead, and Miss Tearsha had held a grudge, even toward Ember. Ember thought it strange that Miss Tearsha's bitterness toward Mamma would infect the whole village, since it was something so personal that happened so long ago.

But Mamma was talking again. "And I'm even more angry that she got you involved. She's hated me for years, and she's entitled. But she's put you in harm's way now, and I'll never forgive her for that."

Mamma touched Ember's hairband again like a good luck charm. They walked along in silence for a while as the light faded. At last Mamma stopped.

"Can you think of anywhere we can spend the night?" Mamma asked. "It's been a long time since I've been out this far."

Ember hadn't come this far often. The last time was during a game of hide and seek. Sean had hidden inside an enormous hollow log and had come out when none of the others had found him. He'd won the game, of course, and they'd spent the next hour sitting together in the log, eating the blueberries Ember had picked when she'd gotten tired of looking. She didn't think it was far ahead, and with any luck, she and Mamma could have blueberries for breakfast.

They found the log easily. It really was huge. One end was totally blocked by the tangled mass of knotty roots; the other was half blocked by a new tree that had grown after the great tree had fallen and had begun to rot out. The hollow space was wide enough that Mamma and Ember could lay side-by-side, if a little too snugly.

Mamma crouched down and peered in. "Give me your bags and put on your cloak."

Ember did as she was told. "What about…creatures?"

Mamma paused and looked up at her. "It's a week after Full Moon, so the only wolves we'll need to worry about are natural ones. Most other creatures won't venture quite this close to a village." She tossed the bags into the dark hollow, then flung her own dark cloak around her shoulders. She got onto her hands and knees and wriggled backward, disappearing into the gap. "Come on," her voice echoed.

Ember slithered in after her. Mamma touched Ember's hairband and pulled up the hood of her cloak, then hugged her close. Mamma's hood was up too. The wool of the cloaks was soft and warm. The past few days and nights caught up to Ember and she drifted off to sleep, her head pillowed on Mamma's arm.

An ear-splitting howl startled Ember awake, and she clung to Mamma in a panic. Ember had felt Mamma jump, and she knew Mamma must have fallen asleep too. Mamma shushed softly in her ear and checked both of their hoods to make sure their faces and hair were fully hidden. Then she held Ember close and listened, breathing softly and slowly. Another howl came, closer this time, followed by an answering call from the other direction. Ember buried her face in Mamma's shoulder. Mamma didn't seem to be afraid, so Ember tried not to be afraid either, but she couldn't stop herself from trembling as the howls got louder and closer. She bit her lips and held her breath when the howling stopped altogether, replaced by snuffling sounds that were amplified by the hollow trunk. Natural or not, wolves had good noses.

The snuffling seemed to go on for hours. The wolves circled the fallen log again and again. They seemed to be confused, able to smell that Ember and Mamma were there but unable to find them. At last, there came a lone bay from a distant voice and the nearby wolves took up the cry, running away toward easier prey.

Ember breathed again, inhaling in one great sob that turned into another and another until she cried herself back to sleep against Mamma's cloaked shoulder.

Mamma shook Ember awake when there was still barely any light coming into the hollow log, but once she was awake, Ember was amazed that she had slept through the racket the early birds were making. She crawled stiffly into the open and stretched as Mamma passed the bags out to her and then slipped through the gap as well. She stretched and gave Ember a big hug.

"You chose a good spot for us," she said. "How about breakfast?" Ember's stomach rumbled loudly. Mamma laughed. "We didn't eat dinner, did we? Were you hungry?" Ember shook her head, yawning. "No, neither was I. Well, we need to eat today. We have a long way to walk."

She opened one of the bags that she had carried the day before. On top, carefully folded in cloth napkins that Mamma and Da had gotten from Grandmamma for their wedding, and that Mamma usually saved for company, were two pasties.

"Where did you get these?" Ember asked, taking the one Mamma handed her and biting into it greedily.

"Mrs. Finnigan brought them over yesterday morning," Mamma said around a mouthful. "She knew we'd forget to cook for ourselves."

By the time they'd finished their pasties, it was light enough that Ember thought she could find her way again. Ember picked up the two bags of yarn; Mamma carried the other three. Both of them kept their cloaks over everything. It was still cool this early in the morning. Ember led the way first to the blueberry patch where they filled their pockets, then back to the road.

They saw no one as they walked. Ember was soon beyond anywhere she'd ever been. Once they were both a little more awake, Mamma started in on Ember's lessons where they'd left off before Da got sick. Most village children were taught by their parents; Ember was only an exception in that Mamma was less strict than other mothers and let her skip lessons to play more often. "We'll make it up another time," was Mamma's excuse, but the time never seemed to come. Now, as they walked, Mamma quizzed her on the trees of the forest and what berries were safe to eat. Ember knew all of those. Mamma had her try to identify birds by their call. Ember got most of those right too. From Mamma's pleased smile, Ember thought maybe Mamma had let her run in the woods so much so that she'd learn these things for herself. It was more fun than sitting inside and mimicking it all back like some of her friends had to do.

"Now," Mamma said, "since we met some wolves last night, can you tell me the difference between natural wolves and werewolves?"

Ember shuddered. "Werewolves are humans who only turn at Full Moon."

Mamma nodded. "For a few nights before and a few nights after, depending on how clear the sky is," she said. "They can still speak in human voices when they are in their wolf form. Like natural wolves, they can bite to kill, but they can also bite to change, making you into a werewolf as well."

Ember shivered and moved closer to Mamma.

"Remember, it's a week past Full Moon," Mamma said gently. "It'll be almost three weeks before any werewolves start to turn again."

Ember nodded.

Mamma changed the subject then. Walking unprotected through the open woods was dangerous, and too frightening a place to learn about nightmare creatures. Ember agreed. They went back to talking about more ordinary things, like ways to start a fire, and how to help green wood dry faster.

They still hadn't seen another person by the time the light began to fade. Mamma sighed. "We'll have to climb a tree tonight," she said. "Can you find a good one?"

Ember scouted a little way off the road for a good resting place, settling at last on a large oak. She and Mamma wrapped themselves in their cloaks and climbed up, perching on wide branches next to each other so that their shoulders were touching. Mamma pulled a hank of something from one of her bags and passed it long-ways around the tree to Ember. It was a light rope of looped and braided yarn. Ember handed it back to her, and Mamma passed it around again, wrapping them to the tree.

"What is that for?" Ember asked as Mamma tied it off.

"For when we fall asleep, or when our limbs go numb, or if something worse happens."

"Is that strong enough?"

"It will hold."

Ember shrugged. Mamma seemed confident in the rope; Ember was confident in her ability to sit for hours in a tree. She'd had lots of practice.

Even though she was almost as comfortable in a tree as on the ground, Ember thought she wouldn't be able to fall asleep. But the day had been long, and they'd walked far. She found herself dozing with her head nodding against Mamma's shoulder. Sometime in the dark of night, she woke, icy cold. If she'd been able to see anything at all, she could have seen her frosty breath. It was late summer, but it felt like midwinter. She shivered closer to Mamma and pulled her cloak tighter around her, snuggling deeper into the hood. She couldn't feel her lower legs, and she couldn't tell if the numbness was from the cold or from staying in one position on a hard tree branch for so long. Hopefully Mamma's rope was as good as she said.

"Mamma," Ember whispered.

"Shh," Mamma said. She reached across with the hand pulling her own cloak tight and held Ember's shivering fingers in her own.

Ember trembled in the silence, realizing as she listened that it was *too* silent. No hooting owls, no rustling from the small night-waking animals looking for food. It was unnaturally quiet, just as it was unnaturally cold. Fear added violence to her shivers. Mamma squeezed her fingers. Ember turned her face to Mamma's shoulder and breathed as slowly and calmly as she could. Mamma had said her rope would hold. Mamma was not shaking with fear. Gradually, so gradually she didn't notice it at first, Ember felt warmer. Feeling returned to her fingers and toes. The air she breathed didn't make her lungs ache. She blinked blindly up at Mamma as she heard the night rustlings beginning again.

"We're all right," Mamma said.

Ember sighed from the depths of her toes and settled back against the tree. She didn't sleep again that night.

They got down from the tree as soon as it was light enough to descend safely. Ember stumbled along, yawning hugely, chewing absently on the two-day-old bread Mamma had packed. Mamma didn't bother trying to teach her much that day, just little bits here and there. At midday, Mamma let Ember take a catnap when they stopped to rest; Ember didn't feel much better for it when she woke up. Mamma kissed her forehead and touched her hairband and they were off again. There was a village somewhere up ahead, Mamma remembered, but she wasn't sure how far, and they both wanted to reach it before nightfall.

The light was just starting to fade when they saw the first signs of human habitation. Trees had been felled to create wide meadows for grazing sheep; in the distance, they could see a structure that looked like a sheepfold or a barn. Mamma took Ember's hand and led her off the road. They picked their way carefully through the field—sheep have no qualms about where they do their business—arriving at the fold just as the shepherds were closing the gate.

"Excuse me," Mamma called before the shepherds could turn and walk away. "Please, is there somewhere we could shelter for the night?"

The shepherds stared at them for a moment. There were three of them, obviously a father and two sons, the youngest of whom was only a couple of years older than Ember. They all had dark red hair and freckles. The younger boy gaped at them.

"O-of course," the father said at last, recollecting himself. "I apologize for our rudeness—you startled us. We are unused to travelers. Please, come with us."

"Thank you," Mamma said.

Ember and Mamma followed the three shepherds on well-trodden paths into the heart of the village. They stopped at a small, neat cottage. Most of them stopped, that is; the older boy burst through the front door without knocking.

"Granny, Granny, we've brought travelers! Travelers have come!" He kept talking so fast that Ember lost the train of what he was saying. His father ushered her and Mamma inside along with his younger son. Ember pulled back the hood of her cloak and looked around. They were in a small but comfortable sitting room with a cheery fire in the hearth. A spinning wheel whirred nearby. The woman at the wheel was so wrinkled and her hair was so silver-white that Ember thought she could be the boys' great-Granny. Her green eyes sparkled at them all, though, and her face crinkled in well-worn smile lines.

"Travelers, indeed," she said. "Did you walk all this way?"

"We did," Mamma said.

"It's more than a two days' walk to the nearest village to the northeast," the shepherd, her son, said.

Mamma nodded. "We spent one night in a hollow log, and the next in a tree." Ember shivered and pulled her cloak around her, even though the room was warm. Mamma put her hand on Ember's shoulder. "We've had our adventures, but we're here and safe now."

"Well, you'll have beds and shelter tonight, and good hot food, too," Granny said. "Nolan, fetch blankets. Craig, Aidan, you two set up mats by the fire, please. You, young lass, what is your name?"

"Ember," she said softly. The old woman's smile was so friendly it was hard not to smile back.

"Well, Ember, you sit by the fire a minute and warm up, then come help me and your mamma in the kitchen. Agreed?"

Ember nodded and crouched by the fire, watching as the whirring of the wheel came to a halt; the old woman got to her feet and led Mamma to the kitchen. The father and oldest boy had disappeared out the front door, and the youngest boy vanished into a back room, returning quickly with his arms full of blankets.

"You're Nolan?" Ember asked.

He nodded. "Did you really sleep in a tree?"

"I wouldn't call it sleeping."

He grinned. "What happened?"

Ember opened her mouth to tell him, but the door burst open just then, and Nolan jumped to help his brother. The three shepherds carried two woolen mats into the room, unrolling them in the corner by the fire. Nolan bent to place folded blankets on each mat. As he did, his brother Aidan tackled him from behind. The two of them rolled this way and that, wrestling, kicking, flipping, and pinning. Aidan talked almost the whole time, a constant stream of taunts and encouragements. Ember tried not to laugh. It was like watching a couple of puppies play. She watched until their father warned them they were getting too close to the fire; they rolled in the other direction, and Ember remembered that she was supposed to join Mamma and Granny.

She went through the door into the kitchen and found Granny bending over a pot of soup on the fire. Mamma had laid her bags and cloak on a chair, rolled up her sleeves, and now was up to her elbows in flour and dough. Ember watched her knead the dough over and over, then cut it into smaller chunks, which she rolled out into long strips. She cut these into little blobs which didn't look like much of anything. Granny peered around Mamma's shoulder and scooped up a handful of the dough blobs and tossed them into the soup. She did this as fast as Mamma could cut them. Ember left off watching Mamma and went to watch the soup instead. The dough ducked and bobbed among the vegetables as the soup simmered. Granny smiled her face-crinkling smile.

"When you haven't time to make biscuits, dumplings are the surest way to feed hungry bellies," she said.

"I love dumplings," Aidan said from the doorway. "Da, can

we stay?"

"Not tonight. Granny's got enough mouths to feed, and your mamma's expecting us home." The boys' father leaned against the door frame and grinned at Granny. "We've righted the beds, and I'll take the boys off before they wreck them again. See you tomorrow!"

"Bye!" Aidan called. Nolan waved as he followed his father and brother back toward the front of the house.

The whole cottage seemed to settle into quiet with a sigh. Mamma cleared the table where she'd been working. Ember moved their bags and cloaks to the beds in the other room, then came to perch on one of the chairs in the kitchen. Granny ladled steaming soup into bowls and set them on the table. Ember could barely restrain herself from scooping out the biggest dumpling and popping it into her mouth while they weren't looking. She settled for blowing on her bowl while her stomach growled impatiently.

At last, Mamma and Granny sat down at the table too, and Granny prayed a blessing on their food. Ember couldn't remember anything tasting quite as good as that first bite. Granny was a very good cook. The vegetables were tender but not mushy, and the dumplings were perfect. The broth was herby and hot, but not so hot that it burned her mouth. Ember ate two whole bowls before she sat back in her chair, feeling sleepy.

Granny led the way back to the sitting room. Mamma helped Ember settle onto a sleeping mat, kissing her forehead, touching her hairband. Granny sat at the spinning wheel again, seemingly able to work by touch alone, because the fire wasn't giving off much light. Ember liked listening to the *whir-whir* of the wheel and the crackle of the fire. Mamma settled herself on a chair. She got out her hook and yarn and her hands began to dance as she talked to Granny. Ember listened sleepily, her eyes half closed.

"You're not afraid here?" Granny asked softly.

"Not tonight," Mamma said.

Granny chuckled. "Do you have a plan of where to go next?"

"No," Mamma said. "I knew of the village here but not much beyond. Can you tell me what lies south?"

"The next human village is at least a week away on foot," Granny said, "or so I've heard. But the road passes close to a vampire hill and through a marsh that is home to wisps. It is not a safe path for a child."

"No."

"There is a house at the edge of the village," Granny offered. "Not much of a house—just one room, quite small—but it has walls and a roof. It belonged to Craig's wife before she married him, and he's been thinking of renting it out or selling it. You might look at it in the morning before you make any decisions."

"Thank you," Mamma said.

Ember found herself hoping that they might stay here in this village. She liked Granny and Nolan and his family, and she didn't want to spend any more nights outside.

The next morning, Granny told Mamma how to get back to the sheepfold. She and Ember wandered through the village, looking around them with wide, interested eyes. To Ember the village looked a lot like the one they'd just left, but there was something different. She couldn't figure out what it was until they were nearly out the other side into the open meadows. She stopped in the middle of the road.

"There's no fence."

Mamma took her hand and towed her along until her feet

got moving on their own again. "No, the fence around our old village is special. Most villages don't have one."

"But what about night creatures?"

"This village has its own protection. It doesn't need a fence."

They found the shepherds in the meadow by the sheepfold. Nolan and Aidan both had pocketknives out and were whittling shapes out of sticks. Their father stood in the shade, keeping an eye on the sheep and the boys. When Mamma told him that she was interested in seeing the house for rent, he gave a short sharp whistle that brought Aidan and a lean black-and-white sheepdog running over.

"Keep watch," he said. He put his hand on Aidan's shoulder and gave another little whistle. The dog sat obediently at Aidan's feet. "I'll be back in a few minutes."

Ember waved to Nolan and followed the adults, glancing back at Aidan and the sheepdog. He stood where his father had, the dog still sitting beside him. She was impressed by how the older shepherd had handed over his authority so easily with just a couple of whistles.

She trotted to keep up as they strode back through the village. Nolan's father—Craig, Granny had called him—talked to Mamma about the house as they went.

"I'm sure my mother told you about it: it's not much to look at, but it's got a sound roof and a fireplace and all," he said. "It's got some privacy too, which you might like."

"That would be nice," Mamma admitted. "I'm not sure yet what our plans are. Would you be willing to let us rent it for one month before we decide?"

"I see no harm in that," he said. "It's sitting there empty. Might as well have someone living in it."

They passed the last cottage in the village and crossed a

narrow creek on a little wooden footbridge. Ember liked the bridge and the giggling of the creek. The house *wasn't* much to look at when they got there a moment later. Craig undid the latches and pushed open the door. Mamma followed him in. Ember hesitated in the doorway. The room was small, with a planed wood floor and whitewashed walls. There was a small hearth in one wall and a window in another. A tiny table that might just fit two people was tucked into a corner with only one stool. And that was it. Ember bit her lip. It was a far cry from what they'd left. But it was much better than walking for another week through a marsh full of wisps and a vampire hill. Ember left the doorway and went to explore the small meadow around the house. There was a little patch of overgrown garden and the remains of wildflowers gone by. She had just discovered a nest in one of the trees at the edge of the meadow and was about to climb up to see what lived in it when Mamma called her over. Craig closed the house back up.

"I need to get some things in the village," Mamma said. "You go back and stay with Mr. Whelan and the boys for a bit, then we'll have lunch with Granny."

Ember nodded. She was glad they were at least going to stay a little while before they moved on. Hopefully a month was long enough that she could convince Mamma not to move on at all.

Nolan and Aidan were wrestling again when they got back to the sheep. The black-and-white sheepdog hadn't moved from his position, still alertly monitoring the sheep, awaiting Aidan's orders. Mr. Whelan surveyed the situation with one eyebrow raised and gave a quick call that came out almost like a bark. Instantly the wrestling match ceased. The sheepdog trotted over to his master, and the boys got up, shame-faced.

"Anyone missing?"

Aidan didn't answer.

"Better count them."

Aidan nodded. He and the dog ran off, with Aidan whistling, chirping, and calling orders the whole time. Nolan tugged on Ember's arm, and together they climbed the tree under which his father stood. From here they could see the patterns the sheep were making as they were herded this way and that. Ember couldn't make sense of it, but every once in a while Nolan nodded approvingly, and once or twice he let out a little snort of laughter at a mistake. After a while the movement seemed to slow down, and their father walked out toward the middle of the meadow to meet Aidan.

Nolan seemed to know this was the end of the show, because he turned to Ember. "So, are you staying?"

"For now," she said. "What were you making earlier?"

He pulled the piece of wood out of his pocket. "It's supposed to be a dog." He shrugged.

Ember tilted her head to the side. "It sort of looks like a dog."

He laughed. "It doesn't yet, and you know it."

She laughed too. "No, it doesn't, but you're the first person I know here, and I want to make friends if we're going to stay."

He turned the piece of wood around in his hands for a minute before tucking it back into his pocket. "It'll look more like a dog eventually. Da is really good at it. He can make a whistle that makes all the same herding calls he makes—other shepherds buy them from him, the ones who can't whistle as well as he can. And he can make sheep that look as real as our own sheep, so real you can recognize them. And once he made a wolf that looked just like A—" He caught himself, as if he'd been just about to say something he shouldn't. "Like a real wolf," he

19

finished.

He looked at Ember quickly. She wondered if Mamma had told Mr. Whelan or Granny about the first night in the hollow log and if they had warned the boys not to talk to her about it. She didn't mind talking about it in the light of day, with Mr. Whelan in shouting distance and the black-and-white dog nearby, but she didn't say anything.

Mamma came back for Ember a little while later. They went back to Granny's, where the spinning wheel was whirring again. Granny's face crinkled warmly when she saw them.

"Your mamma tells me you're going to stay for a bit," Granny said. "I'm glad to hear it."

"Me too," Ember said, going over to stand and watch the wool turn from light fluff in Granny's hands to a thin twist on the bobbin. Granny let her watch for a minute before bringing the wheel to a stop.

"Are you hungry?"

Ember nodded.

The three of them trooped into the kitchen. There were potatoes that had been baking in the coals of the fire, vegetable soup, and even some bacon. Ember ate eagerly, listening as Mamma and Granny talked about the people Mamma had met in the village. They had barely finished eating when the front door crashed open.

"We're here, Granny! What do you need us to do? How can we help?" Aidan called before he even reached the kitchen doorway. Nolan followed along quietly, grinning at Ember.

"You're going to help carry Mrs. Cleary and Ember's things to their new house," Granny told them.

"We really don't need help," Mamma protested. "There isn't much."

"They'll carry the mats and blankets," Granny said, nodding to the boys, who disappeared into the living room.

Ember, now finished with her lunch, started after them. Mamma began to protest again, "Granny, you can't send those—"

"We never get travelers, love, and hard floors are very uncomfortable. You just keep them until you know what you're doing, then give them back."

There was a silence. Ember waited on the other side on the living room door, waiting to hear what Mamma would say. "All right," she sighed. "Thank you. You've certainly helped us to land on our feet here."

"A new place is always hard," Granny said.

Dishes clattered, letting Ember know that the adults were cleaning up and moving around, and she'd better get busy helping. She hurried over to help Nolan hold one of the mats while Aidan tied it in a roll. They'd already rolled the other. They folded the blankets together. By the time Granny and Mamma joined them, the boys were loaded with mats and blankets and were bumping into each other, trying to knock each other's piles to the floor. Their arms were so full they could barely see over the blankets, and they kept tripping over chairs and bumping into the spinning wheel. They were all laughing so hard that Ember was surprised that they hadn't stumbled right into the hearth. She was still giggling as she picked up her own bags and the ones that Mamma had carried from their old home, along with their cloaks. Mamma picked up all of the new things she had gotten in the village that she hadn't taken directly to the house. They said goodbye to Granny, who winked at Ember and cheerfully admonished the boys to be good, then they paraded to the tiny house that they'd be living in for the next month.

Somehow just having Nolan and Aidan there made it feel less empty. They stood the rolled-up mats in one corner to unroll at bedtime, since there wasn't space to leave them open during the day. Aidan opened the window shutter with a jubilant clatter, saw the garden, and ran out with a shout to see if there was anything good still growing. Nolan grinned at Ember and the two of them followed, leaving Mamma some peace. It had apparently been a well-stocked garden once. Vegetables now grew in a rampant weedy tangle and it was impossible to pull one without uprooting another, but they were able to pick a few summer squash and a handful of string beans that hadn't gone by yet. The boys ran off, then, back to their father and the sheep, happily teasing and shoving each other. Ember grinned after them and brought the vegetables back to Mamma.

They spent the rest of the day busily making the house livable. Ember ran about collecting bits of firewood from just under the shadow of the trees around the meadow. Though it was still midday and warm, Mamma made her wear her cloak for this.

"We don't know these woods yet," she said, resting her fingers briefly on Ember's hairband.

Ember shrugged and obeyed.

That night Ember and Mamma ate vegetables from their own garden that they cooked over their own fire in their own house. Mamma had bought bread from one of the women in the village. The house was very empty and very small and in the middle of unfamiliar woods. It was all very new. Ember missed their old house. She missed Da, a lot. She missed running through woods she knew by sound and smell as well as sight. She sniffed and bit her lip as she unrolled the mats side by side. She covered them in blankets and lay down. She watched Mamma sitting on the stool in the firelight, hook and yarn dancing. Ember watched the rhythm of Mamma's hands until her eyes got heavy and she fell asleep.

Ember startled awake in the dark of night. The fire had died down. She didn't know where she was. The room was unfamiliar—the mat, the blankets, the air all felt strange and different. She gasped. Mamma's arm came around her and pulled her close. Ember snuggled against her, breathing her familiar smell, something like spice and yarn and open air. Mamma was still Mamma; Mamma was here, wherever here was... Ember slowly remembered the little house in the meadow and their new friends and watching Nolan running into Aidan with his arms full of blankets. She smiled and relaxed and fell back asleep.

The next day Ember saw more of what Mamma had bought. She had gotten flour from the miller, and now she showed Ember how to make bread.

"I should have done this a long time ago," she said, "but you were having too much fun."

"Am I not allowed to have fun now?" Ember asked, rolling up her sleeves so that her arms were bare like Mamma's.

Mamma smiled sadly. "You are," she said. "I actually think kneading the dough is fun, in a way. But I'll need your help with jobs that aren't fun, too, since it's just the two of us now."

Granny had given Mamma some starter, and Mamma showed Ember how to knead it all together, set it somewhere warm, and let it rise. Ember kept coming back to check on it as she went about her other chores, watching the lumps get bigger and bigger.

Ember and Mamma explored the garden together, trying to

23

figure out where the boundary was with the meadow. They finally gave up and just started pulling what looked like weeds and tossing them into a heap. When they pulled something that turned out to be a vegetable, they set it aside. It didn't take long before they'd pulled enough vegetables to feed them for one day.

"That's enough gardening for now," Mamma said. "We have lunch and dinner. We'll weed some more tomorrow."

Ember was collecting firewood from the fringes of the trees, keeping the little house within sight, when she heard a cheerfully-whistled tune. She straightened up. Aidan was coming across the bridge, hands in his pockets, a hatchet at his belt. He saw her, waved, and headed toward her. He grinned and started talking almost as soon as he was close enough for her to hear him clearly.

"Da sent me to chop some firewood for you, said you'd only have the little branches you could carry from the edge of the trees and that wouldn't last you long or cook you much." His friendly grinned widened as he gestured to the bundle of sticks she was carrying in her cloak. "I know the woods around here, so I can lead you deeper in, if your mamma will let you come with me. I can help you carry more, and I'll split it for you too."

He dashed off to the house to ask for permission to take Ember into the woods, and Ember ran after him, careful not to drop the sticks she'd collected till she reached the side of the house. She dumped them on the small pile she'd started the day before, now nearly gone.

Mamma called Ember to the door. She checked Ember's cloak and touched her hairband. "You want to learn these woods?"

Ember nodded. She didn't like that the woods felt unfamiliar.

She wanted to be comfortable in them the way she was comfortable in her old woods.

Mamma nodded too. "Stay close to Aidan. And don't forget you're supposed to be collecting firewood."

Aidan grinned and ran off into the woods, Ember close at his heels. They wove this way and that through the trees. Aidan wasn't hard to follow, even when he ran a little too fast and Ember lost sight of him for a minute. He never stopped talking. And he always waited for her to catch up, pointing out interesting features before running off again: a large knotted bole, a tree that had fallen and was now leaning in the crook of its neighbor's arm, a stream with perfectly placed stepping stones.

They didn't forget the firewood. After Aidan had led her on what he considered the grand tour, they found a fallen branch that would cook dinner for a week. Aidan whipped out his hatchet and hacked it into manageable pieces, and together they hauled them back to the cottage. It took them a few trips. Ember spotted another good branch on the way, and Aidan cut that one, too. So it went for the rest of the afternoon. Aidan used his hatchet to chop the branches into pieces that would fit in their little hearth, and Ember stacked them beside the house. She was hot and sweaty by the time Mamma called her to wash up for dinner, but she was happy. Aidan's supply of words—and of breath—seemed endless. He had told her about all of the sheep and the people in the village, and laughed at the silly things they had done, until her head was spinning with the names and she couldn't remember any of it. It was nice to sit quietly with Mamma and help her fry the bread—the cottage had no oven—and eat the vegetables they'd collected.

Ember watched Mamma get out her hook and yarn again

when dinner was washed up. She had done it every night for as long as Ember could remember. Ember went over and sat beside the stool to watch. Mamma held the rectangle of work she'd already done and began to add onto one edge, growing it stitch by stitch, flick by flick of the dancing hook.

"What is it called, what you're doing?" Ember asked, finally.

"Crocheting," Mamma said.

"Are you going to teach me that too, like baking bread?"

"Someday," Mamma said. "One lesson at a time, though."

"What are you making?"

"A curtain for the window."

"But we have a shutter."

"We'll want a curtain too."

Ember couldn't imagine why, but she didn't argue. She just kept watching Mamma's hook dance through the loops until her eyes got heavy and the hard work of the day caught up with her muscles. She unrolled the mats and curled up, asleep within minutes.

Nolan arrived the next morning while Ember was plunging into the overgrown garden, pulling the first of the weeds for the day. He grinned and knelt beside her, rolling up his sleeves. She smiled at him and dug her fingers into the dirt, pulling at the roots of the weeds and whatever else was there. One weed was as tall as Ember's waist and so stubborn that they had to work together at it. At last, gasping and panting, they heaved it out. Nolan dragged it to the pile while Ember collected the poor potatoes that had been unearthed in the struggle. They carried these back to the house and washed up in the stream, then Nolan asked if she could go out into the woods again. Mamma gave permission, and Ember grabbed her cloak.

"I offered to come yesterday," Nolan said, "but Da said you'd

26

need firewood, and I'm not old enough to have my own hatchet yet. I suppose Aidan showed you everything?"

"I guess," Ember said. "I mean, we ran all over and he showed me a whole bunch of stuff, but I don't know how much I really saw. I don't think I remember much."

He gave her his ready smile. "I'll show you a little today, and then a little tomorrow, and a little the next day, so that you'll remember it all."

Nolan's smile was contagious. Ember asked, "Where first?"

Nolan was a much quieter companion, and he moved much more slowly, careful not to disturb the woods and the creatures that lived there. Ember liked this. Racing around with Aidan had been fun, but she preferred getting to know the woods the way Nolan knew them, almost becoming part of them himself. They strolled casually, listening. The calls of familiar birds helped set Ember more at ease than anything else had: maybe these woods weren't so very different from her old woods.

They came to the leaning tree Ember remembered from the day before, its neighbor still holding it up in the crook of its arm. She looked at it properly today. Nolan leaned against another tree with his hands in his pockets, grinning as she circled the trees, studying them.

"I dare you to go through," he said when she came back.

Ember shot him a glance then looked back at the pair of trees, two slender birches narrowing together to form a fairy gate. Everyone knew that it was a risk for a human to walk through; you could end up anywhere, or any time, or any*thing*. She looked back at her new friend. "I will if you will."

"Why not? You have your magic, I have mine."

He stood up from the tree, hands still in his pockets, and crossed to the two trees, glancing over his shoulder at Ember, laughing as he passed between them. Nothing happened. Ember, laughing too, ran after him. She felt a little silly, partly for feeling brave for going through and partly for feeling relieved that nothing had happened.

They were still laughing as they turned and started walking home. "I don't know what you mean about magic," Ember said. "But I'm usually pretty safe in the woods. I like the woods, so I guess they like me too." She shrugged.

He gave her an odd look, but said nothing.

Mamma finished the curtain that night. She held it up against the window to look at it, nodded, and set to work on a new rectangle.

"What are you making now?" Ember asked.

"A curtain for the door."

Ember stared at her blankly. "Why?"

"You'll see soon enough."

Mamma's hook didn't skip a stitch as Ember gaped. Since Mamma didn't seem to want to explain anymore, Ember watched in silence then went to bed, puzzling at the mystery until her tired brain fell asleep.

She found herself sleeping more easily each night that they stayed here. She didn't miss Da any less; the ache remained just as great. But when Ember woke in the middle of the night, she remembered a little more quickly where she was. She recognized the touch of the mat and the shape of the house and the feel of the air. She heard the night-noises of woods that were becoming more familiar.

Nolan came back again the next day and the next, just as he'd promised, and Mamma let her have a break from lessons and chores so he could show her more of the forest. The more time she spent with him, the more Ember liked his quiet company and ready smile. Sometimes Aidan came too, and the boys let Ember join their playful teasing as though they'd known her all their lives.

One afternoon, when Ember and Mamma had been living in the village almost two weeks, Ember and Nolan came back into the meadow after an afternoon in the woods. Mamma was sitting on the front step with her hook and yarn, the door curtain on her lap, nearly finished.

Nolan hesitated in the shadow of the trees, watching. "Are you magic, like your Mamma?"

"Mamma's not magic," Ember said.

"Sure she is," Nolan said. "She can do things with yarn other people can't. She's Crafty."

"I don't know what you're talking about. Granny does things with yarn too."

"Not like your Mamma—"

Mamma looked up and saw them. She called to them, and they ran over. Ember was glad of a reason for Nolan not to talk about magic anymore. It reminded her of Miss Tearsha calling Mamma a witch. She didn't want to have to leave this village too.

Mamma possibly being magic didn't keep Nolan from coming the next day. Or the next.

"You ever want to come help Granny sometime?" he asked as they jumped across the stepping stones. They were perfectly placed for a long-legged, growing boy like Aidan or even Nolan; for Ember they were a bit more of a leap.

"Don't you help her?"

"Yep." He took the last longer leap to the bank and steadied himself with his hands in the moss. "Aidan and I take turns chopping firewood and weeding the garden and doing all kinds of outdoor jobs with Da. But she needs inside stuff, too, help with cooking sometimes and with reaching high places when she's cleaning, and sometimes with her wool when her hands cramp." He caught Ember's elbow as she landed on the mossy bank, making sure she didn't slip backward into the stream. "She said she'd pay you in food and yarn." He grinned.

Ember grinned back. She certainly wouldn't mind food, real home-cooked food as a change from what she and Mamma had been making over their little fire from what they weeded out of their garden. And Mamma had been working quickly through all the yarn she'd brought with them. Ember doubted Mamma would mind the arrangement, and she liked the idea of being around the whirring spinning wheel and Granny's crinkly smile.

When they got back to the house, Ember burst through the open door and eagerly explained the idea to Mamma, who was lighting the fire to start dinner. Mamma waited until the tinder caught, patiently feeding it sticks until it would stay lit, then sat back on her heels and looked at Ember.

"That does sound like a nice arrangement, but it'll have to wait another week or two," Mamma said. "Nolan," she added, as he joined Ember in the doorway, "please give Granny our thanks. I'll be needing Ember to help me here at the house for the next few days. I'm afraid she won't be going into the woods again until Full Moon is over."

Nolan nodded solemnly.

"But Mamma—" Ember protested.

"She's right," Nolan said, surprising her. "You don't know these woods yet. Best to be safe until you know them better." He shrugged, nodded politely to Mamma, and walked away, hands in pockets, without the usual bounce in his step.

Ember didn't see why the Full Moon would require so much extra work that she couldn't have a little free time with her friend, but since he seemed to agree with Mamma that the woods weren't safe, she stopped arguing. They prepared dinner, and when they were done eating, Mamma finished the door curtain. Ember could see the moon through their small window as she made up their mats for the night.

"How many nights until Full Moon?" she asked.

"Four," Mamma said. "The effects of the Full Moon begin a few nights before and last a few nights after the night of the actual Full Moon, though they're the strongest on that night."

"So you have to be extra careful of moon-magic for a week," Ember said.

"Exactly," Mamma said. "Which is why I don't want you out in the woods this week, even during the day."

Ember nodded and lay down. She was disappointed, but she understood.

The next day, she and Mamma collected all the vegetables that they could salvage from their weedy garden. Most of them would be all right for a few days inside if they kept them out of the sun. Mamma held out bags of twine that she had crocheted into a kind of stretchy mesh. Ember filled them with vegetables until they bulged, and Mamma hung them in every dark corner of the tiny house. They made bread dough and let it rise, then fried it all in the pan. They put the bread into another twine bag, and Mamma hung this too. Together they filled jars with water from the stream by the bridge and carried them back to their makeshift pantry. Mamma had bought these jars in the village when they'd first moved into the house; Ember had seen them and wondered what they were for.

She still wondered, a little, at the extreme measures Mamma

was taking. They had never done anything like this during Full Moon before. But then, they had always lived in a village protected by a fence, albeit a strange, short one made of wood and twine. Ember thought maybe Mamma felt exposed without the fence, even though she'd said that this village had its own protections.

Once they had enough food stocked up for the week of Full Moon, they brought in firewood, stacking it beside the hearth, just enough to cook their meals. There was no room for more. The small house was looking even smaller, with the extra food, water, and firewood taking up the tiny living space.

Next, Mamma got out the curtains. She pulled the window shutter closed and locked it securely. Then, with a handful of tacks, she and Ember secured the window curtain in place. They tacked each corner and along the sides, leaving no gaps. It made the house feel very stuffy, and Ember thought it would be nice for the middle of winter when they wanted to keep out drafts, but the weather was barely thinking of autumn yet. Mamma was quite serious about it, though, and she hadn't been wrong about anything since they'd left their old village, so Ember held the edges where Mamma told her, and she didn't argue.

They did the same with the door curtain. They tacked it above the door and all down one side. They left the other side and the bottom open for now, so they could still go in and out and let in fresh air, but it, too, would get sealed.

By the time Mamma was satisfied, the sun was nearly setting. Wearing their cloaks, which they'd worn even in the meadow every time they'd gone out that day, they took one last walk around the meadow in the red-gold sunset.

"Time to lock up," Mamma said.

Ember nodded and went inside. Mamma locked the door behind them. Ember helped her tack the curtain across the locked door by the light of the cooking fire. They cooked their dinner, then let the fire burn out. It was very dark. They sat close together on the unrolled mats in the middle of the room. Mamma hadn't taken off her cloak, so Ember kept hers on too. She felt like they were waiting for something, but she wasn't sure what. Mamma hadn't said. Mamma simply sat quietly, listening.

"Ember!"

Ember nearly jumped out of her skin.

"I bet you won't go through the fairy gate tonight!" Nolan called at the window in a half-whisper.

Ember snorted in spite of herself. "I'm not *stupid*, Nolan," she called back.

She heard a muffled scuffle, and then Aidan's voice joined his brother's. "Come on, Ember! There are so many things we haven't gotten to show you yet that you can only see by the Full Moon."

"Not tonight," Ember called, glancing at Mamma.

A long howl split the air in the distance. Ember's blood froze as two more answered, seemingly coming from just outside. She clutched Mamma's arm in the darkness. "Nolan," she gasped. "Mamma, Nolan's outside! We have to open the door and let him and Aidan in before the wolves get them."

Mamma's hands grasped Ember's forearms and held her, kept her from getting to her feet and running to the door. Ember pulled but couldn't get loose, and two hot fearful tears ran down her cheeks.

"Ember, you must listen," Mamma said, her voice low and calm. "Nolan *is* a wolf. Nolan and Aidan are both wolves. They are werewolves. They are *all* werewolves."

Ember froze. She stared at Mamma in the darkness, barely able to see the glint of Mamma's eyes in the dark. "No," she whispered. But Mamma hadn't yet been wrong. And some of the things that Nolan and Mamma had said now started to make sense. "You knew? Why did we stay?"

"Because I knew that with a house like this I could protect us for one week in a month," Mamma said gently. "I didn't know if I could protect us from what we would meet between here and the next village. I didn't even know if that village would be any good, or what we would meet beyond that. The world is not a safe place, particularly for a woman and a child, alone. I decided it would be best to try one month here and see how it went."

"So is it true, what Nolan said, that you can do magic?" Ember asked. She couldn't bring herself to speak of Miss Tearsha or the name she'd called Mamma.

"In a way," Mamma said. "I have something called the Craft. You may have it too—we won't know until you turn sixteen. It enables me to do things with yarn that other people can't. The curtains, for instance, seal the house completely, so that no one can get in, however hard they try."

"And the cloaks?"

"Yes," Mamma said. "There is protective magic in each stitch of these cloaks. They are the reason we survived those two nights in the woods before we arrived here. Your hairband has protective magic too."

"It does?"

"How many times have you gotten lost or hurt in the woods?" Mamma asked.

"Twice."

"Were you wearing your hairband?"

"No," Ember said, remembering, suddenly amazed. "Is that why you made it for me?"

"Partly," Mamma said. Ember could hear the smile in her voice, even in the dark. "I also like seeing your eyes without your hair in your face."

Ember thought about all this for a minute. Mamma's ritual of touching Ember's hairband—it was Mamma's way of checking to make sure that Ember was protected. Ember thought about the twine bags that were holding the food they'd collected for the week. "Is there magic keeping our food fresh?"

"Yes," Mamma said.

She remembered again the fence around the old village. "The fence," she said. "That was Craft magic too."

"It was," Mamma said. "The Craft runs in our family. Your great-grandmamma designed the fence and made it with your grandmamma's help. I wasn't born then. I've maintained it since your grandmamma died."

"And now that you're not there, the fence will stop working?"

"Eventually," Mamma said. "At some point it will start to wear out and break and there will be no one to repair it."

Mamma was still holding Ember's hands, and Ember felt her shrug. The fate of the fence wasn't Mamma's concern anymore.

"Is that why your name is Twine?" Ember asked.

Mamma laughed. "Yes," she said. "Your great-grandmamma had a gift for Prophecy as well, and they knew I would be Crafty. Your grandmamma was proud of the Craft and of the fence they had created."

"Why didn't you name me something like that?"

"Like Wool or Flax?" Mamma laughed. "Because I've learned from my mother's mistake." She paused, and in the silence they could hear more howls, dozens of them, getting louder and louder from the direction of the village. "Now that you know what they are, you understand why I'm telling you we must stay inside. Do not open the door or window—even a crack—no matter what they say, and no matter who says it."

Ember shivered. "I understand."

"It's going to get much more frightening," Mamma said. "Those boys want you to be a wolf pup to run and play with them. They want you to be part of their pack. Same with Granny and Mr. Whelan, but not everyone in the village is that way."

The howls got louder and closer, and Ember could hear human shouts among the howls, though they were still too far away to hear the words. The werewolves' human voices made the whole situation even more awful. Ember huddled closer to Mamma, laying her head on Mamma's lap. Mamma put her arm around Ember's shoulders, tucking blankets over her. As the wolves howled and shouted and called and yelped their way into the meadow around the house, Ember pulled the blankets up over her ears to muffle the sound. She didn't know many of the other villagers yet. She heard only a cacophony of voices, some of them yelling to Mamma to come out, some trying to coax Ember, some hollering suggestions or catcalls at the other wolves, some simply howling at the moon or yipping at each other when human words wouldn't do.

Ember shivered with the blankets over her head for a few minutes before it became clear that it did no good at all. She sat up, curling next to Mamma, their arms around each other.

"Talk to me," Ember said, her voice trembling more than she wanted it to. "Tell me about how the fence was made."

So Mamma told her about how Great-Grandmamma had

designed the fence back in the years when werewolves and vampires and banshees and wisps and all types of nightmare creatures went anywhere they liked. Da's family had been woodcutters, and they had cut the wood for the fence and built its framework.

"There's a gift for woodcraft in your da's family," Mamma said. "You have it already. It's not a magical gift, and your da could have taught you a lot more. He was going to take you as an apprentice in another year."

"Why not sooner?"

"You were having so much fun," Mamma said, stroking Ember's hair, "and your gifts may weigh heavy enough on you when you're older."

The voices outside were getting more and more insistent, more violent in their suggestions. Ember shuddered. She tried not to listen, tried to keep talking, to keep listening to Mamma's calm, confident voice. Mamma was very good at her Craft. Even as the night wore on and they heard scratching, pounding, and hammering at the window, the door, and even at the walls, the house remained secure.

Mamma told Ember about how long it took to learn the Craft, how you couldn't start learning until you turned sixteen and the gift blossomed within you, and then it took years to master, both the stitches of crochet and the magic of the Craft, and the blending of the two.

"You could learn crochet now, if you like," Mamma said. "But you'd have to learn from someone else. I can't do one without the other, so I can't teach you until you're ready to learn both together."

"Did Grandmamma teach you?" Ember asked.

"Yes," Mamma said. "She also taught me to repair the fence.

That was where I met your da."

"Tell me."

"We'd known each other our whole lives, of course—it's not a big village. I was nineteen, and my mother had set me to repair a section of the fence by myself as a test. I was so nervous."

Da had been set to repair the same section, which had been damaged by a recent storm, and the two had run into each other, dropping everything. They'd picked up all their tools and gotten back to work, only to realize that Mamma was trying to stitch her twine with an ordinary stick, while Da was trying to mend the wooden frame with a well-worn crochet hook. They sheepishly returned the tools.

"And that was that," Mamma said, softly. "He looked at me with those rainstorm-gray eyes, and I knew I'd found my home."

Ember remembered those eyes, and she swallowed hard. Da had felt like home to her, too.

They talked through the night, until early birdsong heralded the morning. The raucous villagers howled off home to sleep through the day. Mamma waited until the clearing had been silent for a long while before rising to her feet. She carefully untacked a corner of the curtain and unlocked the door. She peeked out. The sun sliced a sharp line across the house to Ember. Mamma looked at Ember, who looked blearily back.

"We did it," Mamma said. She closed the door again. "Get some sleep."

They lay down and slept through the rest of the morning. In the afternoon, they checked all of their supplies and defenses and walked around the trampled meadow to stretch their legs before hunkering down indoors again. Ember understood now why Mamma had collected everything edible from the garden—the riot of last night had destroyed whatever was left. Ember let her fingers linger on the knotted strings as she got out vegetables and bread for dinner, but she couldn't feel any magic. She wondered if Mamma could feel the magic in them by touch, and if that ability came with the Craft itself once you turned sixteen.

They ate dinner quietly. At last, Mamma said, "Are we brave enough, do you think?"

"Hmm?" Ember asked around a mouthful of bread.

"Are we brave enough to do this every month? There will be another four or five nights until this Full Moon passes, and then every month from here on, at least until we've been here long enough that the villagers get bored and leave us alone."

"I think so."

"And can you still be friends with Nolan, now that you know what he is?"

"Yes," Ember said. She'd thought about it a lot during the day, when the sun had driven away the shadows cast by the moon. "He knows that I might be able to make magic with yarn, and he's still friends with me. It's only fair."

"Then we'll stay," Mamma smiled.

With dinner done, they waited silently for the sun to set outside their safely sealed house. Like the night before, Nolan's voice came first.

"Ember!" he called through the shuttered and curtained window. "I want to show you a place that I haven't taken you before—it's too far to run to between chores, but there's time by moonlight. Will you come?"

Ember swallowed back the part of her that wanted to go and see what he could show her. "Not tonight, Nolan," she called.

"I'll come back tomorrow," he said.

A howl came in the distance. Ember guessed it was Nolan's da calling him home before the villagers came out. His own howl answered nearby. Ember couldn't repress a shiver at the sound, even though she knew it was her friend and that she would still be his friend anyway.

In the silence between Nolan's leaving and the arrival of the villagers, Ember turned to Mamma, a darker shape in the dark house, and asked a question that had gnawed at her all day. "Would it be such a terrible thing to belong to Nolan's pack?"

Even before Da died, it had been just the three of them, set apart. The guardians of the village, Ember saw now. But the way Mamma had spoken of finding home in Da's eyes... Ember didn't think she was alone in wanting to belong somewhere.

"I don't know," Mamma said. "It could be a good thing, to belong to a larger family. But it could be incredibly dangerous. I don't know how the Craft mixes with werewolf magic. I don't know if they've ever mixed before. It could create a power that is beyond our strength to control."

"So we have to stay separate and human."

Mamma nodded. "If, when you turn sixteen, you don't have the Craft, you may decide then to join Nolan's pack. Until then, I have to keep you safe and human."

Howls began in the distance, quickly moving closer as the wolves ran the paths from the village to the meadow around the little house. Ember snuggled close to Mamma. They wrapped their arms around each other.

"Mamma," Ember said, "tell me again about the day you met Da."

The Weaver

Hanna's father was a farmer, if you could call their patch of dirt a farm. He doubled as a woodcutter during years of little rain and poor crops. Her mother kept the house, small as it was, raised the children, and made the food stretch as far as it would go. Hanna was the youngest of five sisters. She knew from watching her older sisters that men wanted to marry women with money or skills, and she would have no money. And to be an unmarried woman in their village… One might as well consider starving to death on purpose or walking naked out into the middle of a blizzard. It was madness.

As soon as Hanna realized that she would need a skill to be useful to a husband, beyond bearing children and keeping house, she began to think what kind of skill she would like. Her mother had taught her to cook and sew, but her cooking was only passable, and she didn't enjoy doing it. So she wouldn't learn to be a baker. Her sewing was somewhat better, but she found it tedious. She enjoyed spinning, but they rarely had wool—only when Father was able to trade for some, and then only enough for one hat or pair of mittens to replace the most worn out item in the house. She loved the feel of it, though. The feel of the cloth was what she liked best about sewing, too. She thought maybe she'd like to weave: to learn to spin wool into thread and turn it into cloth.

The more she thought about it, the better an idea it seemed. So when she was sixteen she told her parents that she'd like to find a weaver to apprentice to, so that she would have a marketable skill when she was old enough to marry.

Her parents thought this was a very wise idea. "You should apprentice with the Weaver herself," her father said. "She is the very best."

"Has she ever taken an apprentice?" her mother asked.

Hanna's father didn't know, but he went out right away to begin asking the neighbors if they knew.

Hanna's mother made her help serve dinner that night. "You still need to learn to keep house," she told her. "No matter how well you weave, your husband will want his house to be comfortable."

No one had been able to give Hanna's father any news about the Weaver. She did not have an apprentice, they were fairly sure, but they did not know if she had ever had one, nor if she ever wanted one.

"We'll have to go ask her ourselves," her father said.

It was nearly planting time, so Hanna's mother had a few more weeks to give her last-minute advice. Most of it Hanna already knew—she'd been watching her mother teach her sisters for sixteen years. When the planting was over, Hanna bundled up what little she had and walked with her father out of the village. The path led up the mountains, through the pass. Hanna had only ever gone a short way along this path before—the best blackberry patch was just above the village. They walked farther up the path, until Hanna, looking back, could see over the roofs of the low cottages. They stood clustered on either bank of the narrow river that cut its way down the valley. They climbed higher, and soon Hanna could see the river more clearly: a long silver ribbon reflecting the overcast sky between narrow strips of flat fields before the land became too steep to farm and the woods took over.

They entered the woods now. Even though it was early in the day, the trees cast deep, green, cool shadows. Hanna's father whistled a tune as they walked. At last they reached a fork in the path. The right path was wider and led steeply uphill, over the mountains. The left path was narrow and overgrown, with branches that reached across to scratch Hanna's face and roots that tripped her. She didn't think the Weaver liked visitors. Her heart began to flutter. Her father stopped whistling.

The Weaver's cottage stood in a clearing. It looked just like the ones down in the village, except that it was built into the side of the mountain. Hanna and her father stood in the sunlight on the front doorstep. Hanna looked around the clearing while her father knocked.

They waited a few minutes in silence. Hanna's father shifted from one foot to the other. He fidgeted with his hands, as if about to knock again, then telling himself to wait. At last he was raising his hand to knock a second time when they heard footsteps. He dropped his hand to his side.

The woman who opened the door was of middling height and thickset. Her hair was once dark, but now it was streaked with silver. Her dark eyes flashed irritably.

"Yes?" she demanded.

"Please, Mistress Weaver," Hanna's father said, his voice shaky. Hanna was impressed he could speak at all. She didn't think she could make a sound. "Would you take my daughter to apprentice?"

"Apprentice?" The Weaver looked startled, then she frowned,

glancing over her shoulder thoughtfully. "That wasn't what I had in mind, but maybe…" She glowered down at Hanna. "How old are you?"

"Sixteen, ma'am," Hanna's father answered for her, when it was clear that Hanna's lips were glued shut.

"Can you keep house?"

"Very well, ma'am."

The Weaver pursed her lips. "Come back after harvest," she told Hanna's father. "If she isn't doing well, you'll take her home."

"Thank you, ma'am."

The Weaver turned her back on them and went into the house. Hanna's father hugged her and kissed the top of her head. Hanna watched him walk out of the clearing, wanting very badly to walk back down the mountain with him now. But this had all been her idea, and she had to give it a try, if only until harvest. She followed the Weaver into the house and closed the door.

It took a moment for her eyes to adjust to the darkness after the bright sunlight of the clearing. There were only two small windows in the front room, barely illuminating the one-person table and single stool tucked beneath one of the windows. Hanna had a vague sense of a cupboard, a chest, and a wardrobe taking up the rest of the room, but the most important thing was missing: the Weaver. She crossed the room and passed hesitantly through the other open doorway.

She froze just inside. The room was three times the size she'd expected. It was brighter too. There were only a couple of windows again, near the wall to the front room. But these windows were bigger, and all of the walls were whitewashed, so the light reflected. She realized as she looked around that it reflected off of other things too—copper frying pans hanging from nails or glass jars that refracted the light into rainbows. At least half of the space had to have begun as a mountain cave, since the shape was less regular at that end. There was a sleeping mat along one wall, a small loom, a spinning wheel, several baskets of wool, and other things that Hanna assumed must be used for weaving, though she didn't know their purpose. But what occupied most of the room was the big loom.

It was as large as the main room of Hanna's family's house, with a dark wooden frame as thick as Hanna's arm. The Weaver sat before it, treadling and passing the shuttle back and forth so fast that Hanna stared, fascinated. The loom was strung with wool in a variety of colors, so that the design looked random at first, but the more Hanna watched, the more it began to resolve itself into small patterns, or a larger pattern, or both. Hanna approached slowly.

"Stop where you are," the Weaver said, when Hanna was still several feet behind her. "You are not to come any nearer than this."

Hanna had momentarily forgotten her fear of the Weaver, but at the sound of the woman's voice, it came rushing back.

"No hands touch this loom but mine," the Weaver continued. "Ever. That is the rule. Can you live by this?"

Hanna nodded.

The Weaver glanced at her. "Good." Her hands stopped their work, and she stood up. She glowered down at Hanna, taking in her appearance. Then she nodded curtly and led the way to the baskets of wool Hanna had seen. "We will begin at the beginning. This wool has already been washed; you will card it."

The Weaver handed Hanna two oddly-shaped paddles with bristles and showed her how to lay the wool across them and brush them together. Hanna tried, awkwardly, to do the same rocking motion that the Weaver had done so deftly, but the paddles felt heavy and clumsy in her hands. At home if they got wool, they picked the knots out with their fingers. She supposed that would take too long here: the Weaver must use a lot of wool in a day.

The Weaver clucked her tongue and took the paddles from her. She demonstrated again. When she finished, the wool ended up straight and neat. Hanna tried again, but the wool came loose in a tangle. She looked up at the Weaver nervously. The Weaver reached out, taking Hanna's hands firmly in her larger ones, and guided her slowly through the motions.

"Keep practicing," the Weaver said. "Lay out your finished wool here." She gestured to an empty space on the shelf, then went back to the big loom.

Hanna stared helplessly at her back for a moment, then went back to carding the wool. By the time the daylight had faded and it was getting hard to see, Hanna had a line of wool tufts on the shelf. She braced herself as the Weaver came over. The Weaver said nothing, sparing the wool barely an unimpressed glance before scooping all of the tufts back into the basket.

"It is time to eat," she said, and led the way into the front room.

Hanna put down the carders and followed her.

Hanna tried to be helpful as they got supper, but she didn't know where anything was, and the Weaver wasn't used to giving directions. When Hanna didn't understand immediately what she wanted or where it was, she often decided it was easier to get it herself. By the time they were eating bread and fried vegetables in front of the fire—the Weaver had brought out another stool—Hanna was feeling very miserable and missing her parents' bright warm house, however small, and her sisters' chatter, and her mother's bossy but clear instructions. Spring seemed a long way away.

After cleaning up supper, they went to bed. The Weaver was not used to company, so she had no extra sleeping mats. She gave Hanna a pair of blankets. "Until you make a mat for yourself," she said.

Hanna looked at her in alarm, but in the dark, the Weaver didn't see the look, and merely lay down. Hanna took her blankets into the front room, where she could mind the fire and look through the doorway see the odd lights and shadows from the faint moonlight hitting the objects in the weaving room. She lay one of the blankets on the floor and lay on it, pulling the other over herself. Hot tears began to roll down her cheek, and she turned on her side and pillowed her head on her arm so that she was facing the wall. She bit her lip and counted as high as her numbers could go, then did it again, and again. She sniffed and wiped her eyes and nose on her sleeve, but at least she wasn't crying anymore. She counted a few more times, more slowly now and more sleepily.

She woke as the early dawn light came through the small windows, reflecting off the copper pan they'd used to make supper last night and right into her eyes. She sat up as she heard the Weaver stir in the other room. They took turns in the outhouse, and the Weaver showed her where the spring was that fed the nearest stream that ran down the mountain. There was a pool farther down to bathe in, but the spring was where she would fetch their water each morning. They carried back a potful of water so that the Weaver could begin making porridge, and Hanna went back for more while it cooked.

After breakfast, they returned to the weaving room. The Weaver showed Hanna again how to card the right way, then left her to it while she wove at the big loom. When she checked on her in the late morning, she again scooped all of the finished tufts back into the basket to be redone. Hanna sighed.

They ate bread and cheese for lunch, and started cooking soup. Hanna stopped her carding every so often to go stir the soup, but it never seemed to burn to the bottom or to boil over. She wondered if there was some magic in the pot or in the Weaver's house; the Weaver seemed to forget that she had anything on the fire at all.

When the light failed that night, the Weaver looked longer at Hanna's tufts of wool, especially the last two, before discarding them. Hanna took this to mean that she was getting better, and hoped that maybe she'd get to keep some of what she did tomorrow.

The soup was good, and the Weaver showed no surprise that it had turned out perfectly. Hanna wanted to ask about it, but instead she knelt beside the Weaver on the brightly woven hearthrug and accepted the bowls of soup she was handed and carried them, mystified, to the table.

The next day was much the same. The Weaver never spoke when she worked, and rarely at other times. Hanna was sure that things would get more interesting after the wool was carded, if she could only get it to come out right; the Weaver's own work still made her forget what she was doing if she let herself get caught up in looking at the patterns. She sighed and tried to pay attention.

She was allowed to keep one tuft that she made that morning, and three from the afternoon. "This is a rolag," the Weaver told her, picking up the one good tuft of wool from the morning. Hanna wasn't entirely sure what made it better than the others, except that the wool maybe held together better, but she nodded. At the end of the day, the four good rolags were put into their own basket with a cloth across the top to prevent them from blowing away. Hanna hoped faintly that she'd learn something new the next day, but she doubted that four were enough.

They weren't. She had another morning of carding before the Weaver nodded and took a wooden spindle from the shelf. It was a flat circle of wood with a stick through the center and a hook at one end. This was a plain spindle. In the boring hours of carding, Hanna had noticed another, more intricately-carved one on the shelf beside it.

"You've used one of these before?" the Weaver asked.

"Yes, ma'am," Hanna said.

"Show me."

Hanna took the first rolag and began to spin as her mother had taught her. It had been some time since they'd had wool at home, and her fingers were slow, but when she finished the rolag, the Weaver didn't look displeased.

"Your form isn't bad," she said. "But your yarn is lumpy. Look." Hanna followed her finger to the spun wool she'd wrapped around the lower end of the stick. There were indeed thicker spots and thinner spots. "Keep practicing until it's even all over."

Hanna spun, carded more wool, spun it, carded more, spun again. She was getting used to her hands aching with tiredness at night. Her spun wool was still too lumpy to imagine that she'd be doing anything different tomorrow. Or the next day, or the next. She got better each time, but attaining an even consistency was harder than she'd expected. She was spinning for most of the week before the Weaver began to show any approval at all.

It wasn't so bad, though. Hanna had always liked spinning when they had wool at home. She didn't like stopping to card more wool all the time, but she was getting better at that too. And it was during this time that the Weaver stopped weaving.

Since Hanna had come to her house, the Weaver had worked all day every day on the big loom, her hands moving almost too fast to see, the pattern growing and changing in mesmerizing ways. At last, she sat back, surveyed her work, and nodded. Hanna watched as she picked up a covered basket and carried it to the spinning wheel in the corner. The basket was full of wool in the same vibrant colors as the ones on the loom. Hanna moved a few steps to the side so that she could see the Weaver's hands, deftly grabbing tufts of wool without looking. She always grabbed the right color, the yarn was perfectly even, and the wheel never stopped spinning.

The Weaver continued to spin the next day, emptying the first basket of dyed wool, then two more. Hanna wondered at the colors: sunflower yellow, leaf green, forget-me-not purple. The Weaver twisted the yarn into hanks when she was done, piling them into one of the empty baskets. Hanna peeked in at them before going into the front room for supper; they were so bright and beautiful.

The next day, the Weaver moved to the smaller loom. It was built like the big loom, but of a more reasonable size. The two looms together took up most of the room, and Hanna had only a little corner to do her spinning. But she got a closer view of the Weaver's work. The Weaver worked too quickly for Hanna to see how she strung the loom, but soon the vertical strands were in place. The pattern that formed across this loom was simple and beautiful, but it seemed flat and lifeless compared to what Hanna had seen taking shape on the other. She blinked at the bigger loom and back at the small one. The colors were the same—yellows and greens, a little red or blue here and there—but they didn't jump out as much. Maybe it was the way the light reflected off all the odd objects to different parts of the room? Hanna frowned.

The Weaver finished this blanket the next day in time for supper, and Hanna watched her cut it down and tie it off, again moving so swiftly that Hanna knew she'd never learn anything here just by watching. For a second, the Weaver held up the blanket, and Hanna got a good view of the whole thing. It was perfect—her father was right, the Weaver was the best. Then the blanket was folded and set aside, and the Weaver looked at Hanna's spun wool from the day.

"Good. Tomorrow I will teach you to use the wheel."

Hanna's heart lifted. She was finally moving on to something new and interesting. She ate cheerfully and fell asleep quickly, having completely forgotten the way the colors in the blanket looked flat and ordinary in a way the other weaving did not.

Spinning on the wheel was a lot harder than the Weaver made it look. Hanna had to keep her feet moving on the pedal in a consistent rhythm so that the wheel would stay spinning at the same speed. She could do it if that was all she was paying attention to, but as soon as she started doing something else, her feet slowed down and the wheel stopped and went backward. On top of that, she had to spin, but the tension was different than with the drop spindle. And the yarn wound itself automatically around the bobbin, instead of her needing to pause and wind it around the lower half of the spindle. That was harder too, because it was much less forgiving and didn't give her much time. She felt hurried, almost panicked, every time she reached for another rolag of unspun wool. When she stopped, out of wool, she looked at what she'd spun. She knew before the Weaver said a word. It was as lumpy as her first attempt with the spindle.

"Practice," the Weaver said. "Move your feet slowly, don't rush. Find the rhythm that sings to you."

That sings to you? Hanna turned that around in her mind as she carded three times as much wool before sitting back down at the wheel. She had no idea what that meant, but she understood about moving her feet slowly. This time she tried to move her feet only half as fast on the pedal as she had before, just fast enough to get the wheel turning. She moved her basket of wool closer, too, so that she didn't have to look when she reached for more. The Weaver was back at the small loom, another blanket already begun, the colors just as flat as the first. She was amiably ignoring Hanna, which Hanna now decided was not a bad way to work: she wasn't talkative and distracting, and she wasn't constantly hovering with advice and criticism. Hanna didn't need the pressure of being watched. Even at a slow speed, her wool was coming out painfully lumpy. At least she didn't feel so hurried, and it was easier to balance what her feet and hands were doing. She was exhausted by midday from concentrating so hard.

Hanna did nothing but card and spin for weeks. In that time, the Weaver made a dozen more blankets. She used the spinning wheel whenever Hanna took a few hours to card more wool, her own yarn coming out smooth and even and perfect, her hands and feet working in perfect unison. Hanna had to constantly remind herself to push the pedal and stretch the wool—pedal and pull, pedal and pull. It did become a rhythm, but it didn't seem to help the consistency of her yarn.

The final blanket came off the loom and was tied off just in time. A man arrived while they were eating their midday meal only hours later. He led a donkey, and the donkey's back was piled high with bags of raw wool. Hanna watched shyly from the doorway. The Weaver looked in each bag, nodding and exchanging a few words with the man before having Hanna help her carry out the blankets while the man unloaded the donkey. The man examined the blankets with a practiced eye, clearly impressed. He nodded and thanked the Weaver, then left. Hanna and the Weaver piled the bags in the corner of the front room and went back to work.

The next day, the Weaver showed Hanna how to wash the raw wool and lay it out to dry. It was a long, body-aching process, and Hanna was soaked from spilling a bucket of cold stream water that she was hauling back to the clearing. When the wool was clean, the Weaver took Hanna out to collect ingredients for dyes. Many plants grew at the edge of the meadow around the cottage—planted, no doubt, by the Weaver herself. Hanna had noticed the bunches of dried flowers hanging from the rafters, but the Weaver didn't have a personality that encouraged questions. They walked into the woods now and into new clearings, and the Weaver spoke softly, pointing out which plants they were looking for, and which to avoid. Hanna already knew poison ivy and poison oak, but she didn't know yarrow or madder. They filled their baskets with flowers; they would come back in a month or two for acorns and walnuts.

The next morning, the Weaver took the largest of the glass jars from the weaving room along with its glass lid. She set it out in the sun on the front step.

"What color would you like your wool?" she asked Hanna.

Hanna thought about the colors she'd seen in the Weaver's work. "Yellow," she said, thinking of the sunflower hue.

Together they took her hanks of messily spun wool and untwisted them, tying them loosely with scraps of string so they wouldn't get tangled. They put the wool into the glass jar with the heads of yellow tickweed flowers, covering it all with warm water and a little vinegar as a mordant. They covered the jar and left it to steep. The rest of the day was spent watching an enormous cauldron over a fire in a pit in the middle of the meadow. The washed wool was put through a mordanting bath first, then drained and put back into the cauldron with various dried flowers in combinations that the Weaver seemed to know by heart. It was Hanna's job to tend the fire, making sure the water stayed just shy of simmering, never boiling. At the Weaver's word, they took the cauldron off the fire and let it sit overnight, removing the wool the next morning and laying it out in the shade to dry.

They repeated the process the next day, and the next. Hanna's head ached from the smells of vinegar and alum and wet wool and the pungent flowers. She checked her jar of wool each morning and evening, but it didn't seem to be changing color very quickly.

"Steeping in the sun takes time," the Weaver said from behind her. "You need to learn both ways."

Hanna nodded and sighed.

Hanna was relieved the day they took the last of the wool out of the dye bath. She went back to her spinning; the Weaver went back to the big loom. Their days fell back into the same pattern as before. When the new dyed wool was dry, they stored it in baskets and bags to be spun later and went back to work. After a fortnight of steeping in the sun, Hanna's wool was ready, and the Weaver helped her to tip the jar out in the meadow, draining the dye. They rinsed the wool until the water ran clear and let it dry. Hanna couldn't help checking on it every so often, just to look at the color. The unevenness of the spinning would make anyone cringe, but the color was so sunny that it made her smile anyway.

Her spinning was improving. By midsummer, the Weaver decided that it was consistent enough that she could start learning to weave. She began by helping the Weaver when she dressed the small loom, setting up the warp threads lengthwise, hooking them through the heddles. She did as she was told, carefully and precisely. She didn't want to have to do it over. When the Weaver approved her work, Hanna went back to spinning and watched the Weaver's hands flick the shuttle back and forth as the blanket grew beneath her hands. When Hanna had helped the Weaver with the warp threads correctly half a dozen times, she was allowed to move on to the next step, learning to treadle and then to throw the shuttle herself. It was similar to the spinning wheel, in that her hands and feet needed to work together, but it was different, too: there was no rush with the loom. She could go slowly, pausing to throw the shuttle, snug the yarn into place with the beater, and then think it through before pressing the next treadle. The Weaver observed silently with a critical eye before going back to the big loom.

Hanna's progress with weaving was no faster than with spinning, but she felt less panicked, and at least she could *see* the progress. She had something to aim for, too, and that was a nice feeling. When she reached the end, the Weaver showed her how to cut the weaving down and tie it off, and watched her dress the loom to weave again. Hanna was weaving with the smoother wool that she was spinning now. Halfway into the second weaving she worked up the courage to ask if she might use some of her yellow yarn as well.

"That isn't smooth enough for weaving," the Weaver said without looking at her. "It will catch against the warp. You will be fighting it constantly, and your final result will be uneven. But the yarn is yours—you may knit with it, if you like."

Hanna got the impression that the Weaver didn't think much of knitting. She thought about this as she wove. Every child in the village was taught to knit, because knitting needles were simple sticks and easy to whittle or borrow. She thought that with that amount of yellow yarn, she could knit herself a sweater, or a dress, or a blanket, or a cloak. Or maybe all of those. She'd been doing nothing but spinning lumpy yarn for *weeks*.

When Hanna finished the second weaving, the Weaver had her lay it on top of the first and sew it up three sides and most of the fourth. Then she stuffed it with wool scraps—bits of spun wool that had been cut from the weaving process, scraps from spinning, knots from the wool removed during carding. She finished sewing up the last side and tied it through with knots in a few places to keep the whole mat together, because that's what she had made: her own sleeping mat, though she hadn't known it until she was sewing and stuffing it. That night, she was almost too proud to sleep on her new mat. She folded the blanket she'd been sleeping on and put it away, knowing she'd need it again once autumn set in and the nights got cold.

Hanna's next weaving was a lesson in changing colors. It had simple stripes of varying widths for the first half; for the second half, she learned to do vertical and diagonal stripes. It was odd looking but warm. She moved on then to a simple design, red on white. Her first time, she misjudged how long the design was and it didn't all fit before she ran out of warp threads. The Weaver let her keep this one too. Her second attempt, she overcompensated and made the design too small. It was otherwise well made, so the Weaver showed her how to cut it down and tie it off early, before it was full-length. It could be a child's blanket. Hanna tried again and again. When she reached the halfway point on her fifth try, she breathed a sigh of relief. The first half looked good. From here, she realized, she could mirror-copy what she'd done for the first half.

When the blanket came down and the Weaver looked it over, she gave an approving nod. "This one can go to the village."

Hanna's heart swelled with pride.

Hanna and the Weaver now took turns on the small loom. Whenever Hanna was using it, the Weaver spun or used the big loom. Whenever Hanna finished a blanket or rug, she took a turn at the spinning wheel for a couple of days so the Weaver could make a blanket. And always in between, the carding. The man who had brought them wool came again just before harvest. He took the blankets they'd made—except Hanna's first poor attempts—and left them with wool and foodstuffs from the village. Hanna thought, watching him leave with his poor donkey weighed down with blankets, that it would have been easier if the Weaver had lived closer to the village. She'd wondered many times why she didn't, but she never dared to ask. She assumed it must be because the plants used for dying were easiest to find here, and the Weaver wasn't much for company.

Hanna's father came back after harvest. Hanna had decided

by then that if the Weaver would let her stay, she wanted to. She liked the feeling of the wool, and watching patterns form as the weaving grew. She even liked spinning and dyeing, though she was glad they didn't do the dyeing very often. The Weaver had never expressed an opinion on the trial, though, so Hanna's heart was in her throat as she opened the door at her father's knock. She hugged him and pulled away quickly, her eyes welling up. She hadn't expected to be so overwhelmed by his familiar smell of wood and sweat and garden soil, or the way he hugged her shoulders tight with one arm. She gave him a crooked smile.

"Wait right here—I'll tell the Weaver. And I have something for Mother."

She ran across the front room to the doorway of the weaving room and poked her head in. The Weaver hadn't moved from the big loom. She had to know that it was Hanna's father; no one ever visited, and this was when she'd told him to return. Hanna told her who it was, then dashed the cupboard in the front room where the Weaver had given her a little bit of space for her own. She'd folded one of her blankets here, and all of her hanks of yellow wool. The best were in front. She took them out and latched the cupboard, returning to the door just as the Weaver arrived. Her heart raced as she hovered in the doorway.

The Weaver stepped out into the spring sunshine. She wasn't much shorter than Hanna's father. "She learns well. I'm willing to keep her if you're willing to let her stay."

Her father nodded slowly and looked up at her in the doorway. "Hanna? Do you want to stay?"

She nodded, too relieved to speak.

The Weaver nodded abruptly and returned into the cottage.

"Say your goodbyes, then," she said to Hanna as she passed.

Hanna gave her father the sunny yellow yarn to give to her mother. "It's a little uneven," she said, blushing. "I'm better at it now."

"It's beautiful," her father said. He kissed her forehead, blinked, and walked out of the meadow.

Hanna stayed with the Weaver for two years. She learned to weave with multiple colors and with different textures. As her old dress wore out, the Weaver showed her how to weave a lighter cloth and sew a new one. When they traded finished blankets for wool and foodstuffs, more of the blankets were now Hanna's. Though she didn't fool herself that anybody looking couldn't tell the difference, she was still proud of her work.

But she was never allowed to touch the big loom.

She was never even allowed within a few feet of it. The weaving on that loom was never cut down and tied off, was never begun again. She had no idea how the warp threads kept going, because they seemed to continue endlessly. Sometimes, when she had finished a weaving or whatever spinning she was doing that day, she would stand and watch for a few minutes and study the patterns, letting them get inside her as they seemed to do, tangling and untangling among themselves as they formed a larger design. She felt that if she could understand the design on the big loom, she'd understand all patterns.

After one year, when the Weaver had not criticized anything in her last three blankets, she asked the Weaver when she might be taught the big loom.

"You're not ready," the Weaver said.

Her answer rankled Hanna, because it didn't seem to be an

answer at all. Of course she was not ready *yet*, but she had hoped she might be told when, or even what she still needed to work on first.

When the weather was reliable, the Weaver sometimes sent Hanna on errands to the village, for food they did not grow or get in trade from the man with the donkey, or when something broke that they could not fix themselves. She always stopped to visit her family and said hello to the friends she'd left behind. But after the quiet of the Weaver's house, the village felt loud and bright and overwhelmingly full of life. It reminded her, in a way, of the Weaver's weaving, the one that never came off the big loom, particularly when she paused to look at the village from above, a short way up the path. There were little patterns for individual people and families, but they all came together into one larger design that was the whole valley, and the river ran through it all. Hanna smiled as she thought this; she must be turning into a real weaver now, if she was seeing all life in terms of patterns in wool.

She studied the big loom more after this, both to see if it really did look like her idea of village life, and because of the Weaver's comment. She wanted to prove that she was ready, somehow. Maybe she could tell the Weaver the pattern or recreate it on the small loom. She was approaching her eighteenth birthday, and her friends in the village were courting or already married. Her parents had mentioned at her visit last fall that perhaps she had learned enough from the Weaver to return home. She knew they were right; she had enough skill with the loom to provide for a family of her own. But she knew that she would not be satisfied if she did not learn the secrets of the big loom, so she put them off, telling them that there were still things the Weaver was teaching her, to give her another six months.

She was five months into that time in early spring when the warp beam of the small loom broke. Hanna had been in the middle of using the small loom when there was a resounding crack and the tension on her work went slack. She and the Weaver both stared at the beam in shock and dismay—it had nearly snapped in two, just to the left of center. They dismantled the loom and took the warp beam down, carrying it gingerly so that it wouldn't break more. The Weaver chose to go to the village herself to oversee the repair. She breakfasted with Hanna early the next morning and left, Hanna sitting at the spinning wheel with baskets of wool to occupy her day in the absence of the loom.

Hanna spun for about half an hour, waiting for the Weaver to be well on her way, before she rose and approached the big loom. She studied it for a long moment. She was sure she knew the pattern; she'd been a few inches into replicating it on the small loom when the warp beam broke. Heart racing, Hanna glanced at the door and sat down on the Weaver's stool. There were more treadles on this loom, but she was sure she knew the right order to press them—she'd memorized the motion of the Weaver's feet. She picked up the shuttle and carefully began to weave the next piece of the pattern.

An inch into it, she could see that something was wrong. The blue was getting a little out of place. She tried to tweak it back, but the next row was worse. She didn't mean to keep going, but her hands now wove out of habit. Hanna watched in sick fascination as the fabric grew, the blue spreading until it interfered with all of the other small patterns, unsettling the whole design. With a small cry, she pushed herself back from the loom, toppling the stool. She stood back where she'd always looked at the loom and gaped at it, panting. How had it gotten so out of control? She'd never had that happen with a pattern before. It was as if the colors had minds of their own.

Hanna glanced over her shoulder at the door again. The Weaver wouldn't be home for hours yet. She had time to fix this. Hanna took a deep breath. She had to undo everything she'd just done. She stepped up to the loom again, leaving the stool on its side. But when she went to move the shuttle backward, to unweave it all, it wouldn't go. She tried again. She picked at the thread and pulled on it from the other end. It pulled loose but not out. She tried another color. The same thing happened. All she managed after twenty minutes of trying to unweave her work was to create a massive tangle.

Hanna sat on the floor in front of the loom, panicked tears pouring onto her lap. She wasn't supposed to touch the loom, she wasn't ready, now the Weaver would *never* think she was ready. How was she supposed to fix this so the Weaver wouldn't know? She wiped her eyes on her sleeve so she could look at the loom clearly. If she could only take it out back to *there*, where the blue had begun to go wrong. She got up and loosened the row as best she could. She stared at it, frozen, for a long moment, then got the scissors and carefully cut one strand. Her heart stuttered as she did this. She hoped she could tie it back together with a knot the Weaver wouldn't notice. With the strand loosened, she was able to untangle it from the others with no trouble. She breathed a little easier. She cut another, and untangled that, then another. Seven strands she cut, and she had the knot nearly undone and the mess she'd made almost unwoven.

The door crashed open. Hanna whirled, heart stopped.

The Weaver was out of breath, her face red from hurrying back up the mountain. "What have you done?" Her voice was hoarse.

Hanna opened her mouth helplessly. There was no hope of lying or hiding what she'd done. Somehow the Weaver knew. So she told her everything, from how she'd tried to replicate the pattern on the small loom to how the blue went wrong to how the whole thing tangled when she tried to undo it so she'd had to cut threads. "I'm so sorry," she finished. "I almost have it out now."

"Stop, girl, step away!" the Weaver snapped, striding forward. "You've caused enough harm already!"

Hanna leapt away from the loom like a startled rabbit. She stopped against the wall by the spinning wheel, quivering. The Weaver, very carefully and in complete silence, tied off the cut ends of the seven strands. Then she slid the rest of the rows of weaving back down onto the row where Hanna had made the cuts. Hanna was surprised to see that she was weeping. The Weaver unknotted the tangle with gentle fingers, painstakingly loosening a thread here and a knot there until all of the remaining colors were free. Hanna looked at what was left of her attempt to work on the big loom and gulped—mostly blue and brown, with little bits of the other colors showing through, but not much, and huge gaps where the warp threads could be seen where she'd cut and unwoven the seven strands.

Hanna had piled the threads she'd cut on the righted stool; now the Weaver turned to these. She wound each color around her fingers and tied them into a tiny skein, tears rolling freely down her cheeks as she did. Hanna watched as she picked up all seven of them in her hands and held them against her heart, her tears dripping off her chin and onto her cupped hands. The Weaver began to hum as she found a white, woven square only a few handsbreadths wide. She placed it on the stool and piled the tiny skeins in the middle, folding the woven cloth in on itself until it hid the colors completely. Hanna's throat felt tight; there were no words in the Weaver's song, but it was clearly one of mourning. She followed the Weaver as she went outside, watching from the doorway as the Weaver took a trowel from their dye-gathering tools and dug a small hole in the newly-thawed ground at one edge of the meadow. She buried the cloth that held the cut strands, humming the whole time. The song had ended when the last scoop of dirt had been placed back in the hole. She didn't look at Hanna as she reentered the house, and Hanna backed up into the shadows behind the door to let her pass.

The Weaver returned to the big loom. She ignored the stool now; she sat cross-legged on the floor in front of the loom. Just sat. Hanna sat too, in her spot against the wall behind the spinning wheel, where she was out of the way but she could still witness. She had done something horribly wrong. The Weaver had told her when she'd first arrived that nobody touched the loom but the Weaver herself, and she'd done it. But it was obviously worse than that, or the Weaver wouldn't be grieving so strongly. A person doesn't grieve over a mess in a weaving, or over a tangle. Hanna had made enough mistakes in her own weavings to know this; even the Weaver had made a mistake or two in the time Hanna had been there, on the small loom, and she had fixed them and moved on. This was not like that. Hanna remembered too clearly how the threads on the big loom would not pull out, would not unweave. She hadn't been able to undo what she'd woven. The secret of the big loom was bigger than just an overly complicated pattern, or of a weaving that never came down. She shivered.

They stayed like that all night. When it got too cold, Hanna got the blankets from their sleeping mats. She draped the Weaver's around her shoulders, not expecting any acknowledgement so she wasn't upset when she didn't get any. She wrapped her own blanket around herself and sat back down against the wall and waited, keeping her own vigil. She didn't understand what was going on, but it was her fault.

When day broke, the Weaver stirred. She stood creakily, folded her blanket and set it back on her mat. She went out, and Hanna didn't follow. She stretched and folded her own blanket instead. In a moment, the Weaver returned, her face clean of tears and red from the cold stream water. She pulled the stool up and sat at the loom, studying it carefully for a moment, then she began to weave.

Hanna watched. The Weaver's hands were slower than usual this morning, whether because of the early morning or the cold water or the long night's vigil, she didn't know. Maybe the Weaver was still thinking as she worked how best to bring Hanna's mess back into alignment with the pattern as it was and should be. Hanna sighed. The Weaver worked for the whole morning without saying a word. Hanna ought to have been spinning, but she couldn't. She could only watch. The Weaver paused for a bit of bread and water at noon, but only because Hanna brought them to her. The Weaver gave her a long look, then nodded curtly, took what was offered, and went back to work as soon as she was done. Hanna cleaned up what little she'd gotten out in the front room and came back again to watch.

The Weaver did sleep that night, but the next morning she was up with the dawn and back at the loom. She spoke to Hanna for the first time since she came home, startling Hanna. "You said you tried to weave this design on the small loom?"

Hanna nodded, cheeks reddening.

"Foolish girl. No wonder it broke. That loom was not built to hold it." The Weaver's hands continued their work, faster now than the previous morning. Hanna noticed that she had added in a new color or two. "I had to leave the warp beam beside the path halfway down the mountain. You must go today to get it repaired. I can't leave this now, and the beam can't sit out in the weather."

"Yes, ma'am," Hanna said. She was torn between wanting to keep watching the Weaver work—how were the new colors going to change the pattern?—and wanting to get out of the house, away from the big loom and the ugly blue-brown stripe across the Weaver's beautiful pattern. But it was her fault the Weaver had had to leave her errand unfinished, so she took her winter cloak from the peg in the front room, since spring was still very young, and began her walk down the mountain.

She nearly missed seeing the beam. The Weaver had left it alongside the path where the trees opened out and the ground fell away steeply. It had always been one of Hanna's favorite views of the valley, and she usually paused here to look out. Today she stood frozen, horrified. The river, usually placid and reflecting a blue-gray sky, now roiled high over its banks, muddy-brown and violent. Mud and rubble showed where the river had been even higher before, snapping cottages like matchsticks in its snow-swollen rush. Hanna stumbled forward, hurrying to see her family and whether she could help, and she tripped over the piece of wood on the ground. For a second she was startled to see it there, and then she remembered why she had come out that day at all.

She rushed down the rest of the way. By the time she'd reached the valley floor, she decided to do the Weaver's errand first; the beam was heavy, and she didn't want to put it down somewhere and forget. So she went to the home of Ari the carpenter, who repaired just about anything, and to whom she'd brought other broken bits for the Weaver over the years. He lived at the foot of the hills, close to the river but not so close that his house was in danger. She found him standing at his door, watching the wild water with a frown.

"Worst flood I've ever seen," he said when he saw her, as a form of greeting. "There're floods every few years—a 'specially bad one when I was a lad—but never like this." He took the beam she handed him. "Broken loom, eh? Never seen one of the bigger pieces break like this. Some week. I'll have it fixed for the Weaver within the fortnight."

"Thank you," Hanna said, turning to go.

"Don't you go into the village," Ari warned. "Water's still unpredictable, and odd mudslides are causing trouble. Seven people have died already. Let's not make it more."

Hanna's face went white. Her heart froze. Seven?

Ari saw her reaction and put a reassuring hand on her arm. "Your family's safe, child, all of them. None of them live close enough to the water for fear."

Hanna nodded vaguely, but there was a strange ringing in her ears.

"Best you go home to the Weaver now."

Hanna nodded again. She turned and walked back the way she'd come, not pausing or looking back until she reached the place where she'd first seen the flood. She turned then and gazed over the valley, her pulse now thundering in her ears. The Weaver had seen something right here that had made her turn and come rushing back. Hanna herself had thought, looking down at the valley from this place, that life in the valley seemed to make a pattern similar to that on the big loom. A muddy river overflowing its banks—blue wool and brown, out of control. Seven people dead. Seven small skeins of cut yarn, buried in the meadow.

Bile rose in Hanna's throat and she retched.

She didn't return to the Weaver's house right away. She was sure the Weaver didn't expect her to. But she couldn't bear the sight of the river either. She moved up the path a little farther, into the woods where the trees would block her view, then found a fallen log. There she sat and sobbed. She cried until she was shaking and exhausted and cold. The sun was going down. She stood up and walked the rest of the way to the cottage.

The Weaver was kneeling before the fire in the front room, stirring a pot of soup. "You should eat," she said.

Hanna wanted nothing to do with food, but she took the bowl she was handed. "Ari will have the warp beam mended in a fortnight."

The Weaver nodded. "You may spin until then. There is also dyeing to do."

Hanna cringed at how "dyeing" sounded like "dying." She moved the vegetables around in her bowl with her spoon, watching the Weaver eat. How could she eat and sleep, knowing she held the lives of these people in her hands? Did *they* know? Surely not. Hanna hadn't, and she was sure her father would never have apprenticed her to the Weaver if he had.

They cleaned up and went to bed, the Weaver now acting as though nothing had happened. Hanna lay on her mat, listening to the Weaver's breathing. She couldn't pretend everything was normal. She couldn't stay here with that loom, and she couldn't learn to use it. She couldn't wield that kind of power. She swallowed down bile just thinking of it.

When she was sure the Weaver was asleep, Hanna got up. She rolled up her sleeping mat and folded her blankets. She got her yellow yarn from the cupboard. This was all she owned, besides the threadbare dress she'd arrived in. She tucked the blankets and the yarn inside the dress, along with a loaf of bread and some cheese that she found by feel in another cupboard. She twisted the whole thing around the sleeping mat and tied it on itself with the sleeves. Pulling on her cloak, she picked up her bundle and slipped out the door.

There was a three-quarter moon, just enough to see the path but not much besides. Hanna's eyes adjusted quickly to the dark. She was tired—she hadn't eaten or slept much in days, but she didn't think about that. When she came to the place where the overgrown path from the Weaver's cottage met the wider path over the mountain, she hesitated. Her parents had been urging her to come home. She could get married; she had learned a skill.

Hanna turned her back on the valley and treaded upward, over the mountain. She couldn't stay in the domain of the big loom. She couldn't live the rest of her life looking at the river that she'd flooded, surrounded by the families of the seven people she'd killed.

Hanna walked through the silent forest, the wide path ahead a pale swathe in the moonlight. When the moon set a few hours before dawn, she wrapped herself in her blankets and huddled in a small hollow just off the path, hugging her bundle, and slept fitfully until dawn birdsong woke her. She ate a little bread with a dry, sticky mouth and kept walking. She had no plan, no direction but "away," but that carried her for four more days of walking. She passed the first two villages without a second glance—if she stopped too close, they would find her easily. She ran out of bread sometime in the third day, but she'd learned enough of foraging to find some early berries.

The walking brought her a kind of clarity. She couldn't go back; this was clear, had always been clear. But she saw that the Weaver had sent Hanna to the valley not only to repair the small loom but to learn the truth of what she'd done firsthand. The Weaver knew it was a horrifying thing, the power the loom had over the valley, and she felt it strongly still—that's why she'd mourned first, before she'd begun to repair the flood damage. But she'd made her choice, and by returning to normal life, she'd offered Hanna the same choice. If she had chosen it, Hanna could have stayed, and perhaps knowing the truth was what made one ready to learn to work the loom.

But she could not have stayed. To have that power over her village, over her own family… Hanna wondered suddenly if the Weaver had family down in the valley, and whether any of them had been among the seven. She shivered.

Dusk was falling on the fourth day when Hanna reached another village. She was so tired and hungry that she had made up her mind to beg some food and sleep in someone's barn before moving on. She stopped at the first door and knocked. A young girl of eleven or twelve opened it. She looked well-fed and cheerful. She froze at the sight of Hanna, and the two girls stared at each other for a minute, Hanna too exhausted to speak.

"Who is it, Evie?" came a woman's voice from inside.

"A girl," the young girl called over her shoulder.

"Well, invite her in," the woman's voice said. "Remember your manners."

70

Evie stepped back and opened the door wider, still staring.

Hanna took the implied invitation and stepped inside. The room was cozy and lit rosily by firelight and candles. As Hanna looked around, her jaw dropped, and she almost burst out laughing. There was a spinning wheel surrounded by baskets of wool in one corner, and a young woman sat at a loom—a normal-sized loom—in the middle of the room. Another small loom stood off to one side. The young woman rose and came over to Hanna.

"Welcome," she said. "I'm Minna, and you've met my apprentice Evie. How can we help you?"

Hanna opened her mouth to answer and caught a whiff of something cooking over the fire. Her stomach rumbled loudly. She blushed. "My name is Hanna," she said. "I was wondering if you might be able to spare some food and a place to sleep."

"Of course," Minna said, smiling warmly. "You'll stay here with us tonight."

Evie took Hanna's cloak and bundle, and Minna went to check the stew. While she waited, Hanna examined the weaving on the loom. Minna was very good—not as good as the Weaver, perhaps, but then, the colors in the weaving were also reassuringly flat and ordinary. They sat down to eat, and Minna and Evie chatted cheerfully, including Hanna in their conversation, though her mouth was usually too full to say much. But she liked listening to them, and she thought that, on closer observation, Minna couldn't be more than five or ten years older than herself. By the time she'd finished her stew, she was talking and laughing with them, and she'd almost forgotten where she'd come from—almost, but not quite.

After tidying up, Evie went straight to bed in the next room. Minna invited Hanna to sit by the fire with her first. Hanna wondered if she'd waited until Evie was out of the room to start asking awkward questions. She steeled herself.

Minna looked at her thoughtfully. "I don't know how much of a hurry you're in to get to where you're going, but if you'd like to rest here another day, you're welcome to stay."

Hanna blinked at her. She hadn't been expecting that at all. "Thank you," she said. "I...don't know where I'm going. I can help tomorrow—I'm a weaver too." She paused, then found herself wanting to tell Minna more. "I was apprenticed to a weaver but I had to leave when my village was flooded," she said carefully.

Minna nodded. "I was wondering if you were walking away from something rather than toward. If that's the case, you can stay as long as you like. As I've said, it's just me and Evie—my husband died of a fever only two years into our marriage, and I kept myself by my weaving. Evie was orphaned last winter, so I took her in." She paused. "I don't need another apprentice, and I'm guessing you don't need to be one anymore, but you could be my assistant in exchange for room and board."

Hanna nodded, a shy smile spreading across her face.

Minna led her to the second room where she lay out her sleeping mat beside the others and stretched out on it. She was exhausted, and it was so nice to be warm and indoors again. But even as she was relaxing into sleep, she took a minute to just be hopeful. From the dinner conversation, she thought that it would be a fun change to live and work with Minna and Evie—they were young, and lively, and talkative, and she expected that they might sing and laugh while they worked.

Slipknot

When Breann got home from work, Paul was gone.

She stood just inside the front door of the house, frowning at the place where his shoes should have been. He'd gotten up early that morning, she remembered, slipping out of bed at the first hint of a beep from his phone alarm, silencing it before it could disturb her. He'd kissed her on the forehead. She'd rolled over and tried to mumble something between "goodbye" and "I love you." It was still dark, still an hour before her alarm would go off. He was going for a run in the woods out back before he had to get ready for work.

She'd overslept that morning, hitting snooze three times too many, and he'd already left for work by the time she'd come downstairs. Or so she'd thought. Now, after work, she worried that maybe he hadn't come home from his run. The thought gave her chills. Had he been lying in the woods all day, injured? She stood frozen, twisting her wedding band around her finger. It tugged oddly as she twisted it. She'd done Gram's trick because Gram had just passed and it was a way to remember her by. She never thought she'd need to *use* it.

Breann began to move through the house, grabbing things out of each room as she went. She dug an old backpack out of a closet and filled it with granola bars and water bottles from the kitchen, the first-aid kit, and a flashlight from the garage. On a whim, she threw her knitting notions pouch in the bag—the pouch had tiny scissors, needles, and safety pins, among other things, and you never knew when you might need those. Then she went to the bedroom to change, throwing on jeans and a t-shirt, and after some debate, two sweaters. It was surprisingly warm for the end of October, but it got cold at night, and she thought she'd heard something about snow in the forecast. She pulled on thick socks and sneakers, then went back downstairs.

It was tempting to pick up the backpack and run out the door, but Breann forced herself to make a peanut butter sandwich and eat it, looking out the kitchen window at the backyard toward the way she was sure Paul had gone. She hadn't had time to eat much at lunch, and she wasn't sure when she'd have a chance to eat a real meal again. Now that she was standing still, she was able to feel the slight tug on her wedding band even when she wasn't twisting it. It was tugging in the direction of the side door, which was the door he usually used when he went out in the early morning, since it closed most quietly. She shivered.

Gram had taught Breann to knit when she was fifteen. She'd just had her wisdom teeth out and was miserable, and she had to stay with Gram while her parents took her older sister to college orientation. To combat her restless boredom, Gram had handed her a pair of needles and yarn. She'd taken to it like a fish to water.

"It's in your blood," Gram had said. Gram was from northern Scotland, and her mother and mother's mothers for generations had been knitters.

When she taught Breann how to knit her first sweater, Gram leaned close and said, in the lilt that hadn't gone away, even after decades of living in the States, "I'll teach you a trick, love." At the end of the sweater, instead of cutting the final thread and sewing it under, Gram took the work from Breann's hands. She tied a slipknot in the yarn and then tied the other end of the yarn to her wedding band, the one she still wore from Grandad, who had died when Breann was too young to remember him. Breann blinked. The yarn didn't quite disappear; she could still see it if she was looking in the right place. But almost.

"What did you do?" she asked.

"A trick my mother taught me," Gram said. "All the women in our family know it, and now you do too. You knit a sweater for your man to wear when he goes out fishing, then you can follow the yarn if he doesn't come home."

"You mean…drowned?" Breann made a face.

"No, love. Where we're from, the fae folk live in the sea and swim with the fish and the seals, and sometimes they'll lure a man away to live under the sea with them. If a woman is brave and cunning, she can go after him and get him back."

Breann had stopped believing in Gram's stories about the fae folk when she was a child; at any rate, they didn't seem to live in New England. She turned the conversation back to her boyfriend. "Paul's not a fisherman."

"Still, love, it's a good trick to know."

And for whatever reason, Breann had remembered the lesson. Years later, after she and Paul had gotten married, she knit him a sweater, and she couldn't quite bring herself to cut the final thread. Maybe Gram's funeral was too fresh in her memory, but Breann found herself tying a slipknot instead and tying the other end of the yarn to her wedding band.

"Not that it matters," she'd muttered to herself. "He's an accountant, and we're not in Scotland." But it gave her a little thrill to watch the yarn seemingly disappear.

Now she finished her sandwich and put her plate in the sink. Before she picked up the backpack, she fumbled with the bottom edge of her second sweater. It was the latest one that she'd knit, a chunky dusky blue, and she was able to find the final stitch without too much trouble, but it took a little work to get the end unraveled. Once begun, though, a short tail unraveled nicely. She picked up the backpack and walked out the side door, locking it behind her.

She hesitated, not sure if this would work. She made a slipknot in the tail she'd just unraveled from her sweater and tied the other end to the doorknob of the house. The yarn faded slightly, but not quite as much as it had with Paul's sweater. The trick was probably not meant to work on houses. Oh well. She turned and started jogging in the direction that her ring was tugging, across the backyard, up the hill and the short logging road into the woods. Reddish-gold sunset light fell in patterns between the trees. Breann paused when the tug on her ring told her to cross a stream, looking for the driest way, and glanced down. Her sweater was unraveling. Already the three inches of ribbed edging were gone. The yarn that stretched back toward the house was still nearly invisible in the dusk. She bit her lip, mourning the loss of all that work, but she'd found the stepping stone she wanted. She jumped the stream and kept going.

At this point she had to get out the flashlight, because after jumping the stream the yarn trail left the logging road. She tried to step lightly through the underbrush, but twigs snapped and dry leaves crackled with every step. She walked on and on, ducking under branches, tripping on roots, stifling cries of alarm when something skittered nearby or flew too close overhead out of the darkness. Every time she had to stop to free herself from the twigs that had caught her sleeve, she noticed how much shorter her blue sweater had gotten. Her other sweater, pale lilac, was visible from her midriff down.

The yarn trail stopped unexpectedly. Breann had sidestepped the massive trunk of an ancient tree and suddenly realized that the tug on her finger was coming from a different direction now. She backtracked, shining the flashlight across the forest floor as though she might catch a glimpse of sage green wool. Nothing. The tug on her ring led her to the foot of the giant tree and then ended. Breann shivered. Echoes of Gram's stories whispered through her mind. She backed away a few feet to where she could hide behind a fallen log and still keep an eye on the tree. She turned off the flashlight. The darkness was almost complete. She could just make out the tree's outline.

Breann wasn't sure how long she crouched in the darkness. She was hungry again, but she didn't dare move. The night was lit by nothing but stars. Breann could see some of the star-spattered sky through the skeletal branches, but there were enough pine trees in these woods that no real light got through. She hadn't been out this late at night since she started working full time, and she'd forgotten how far they were from light pollution out here.

A twitch of the yarn on her ring drew Breann's attention back to the tree. Her mouth fell open. A crack had opened in the trunk, about as high as her mid-thigh, forming a sort of doorway, through which a faint silver light gleamed. Everything was completely silent. She couldn't see any people coming or going through the doorway; they may have slipped through before she'd noticed the door was open. She crept out from behind the fallen log and crawled through the gap, wriggling sideways a little as her shoulders and hips caught on the tree.

The doorway led to a long downward tunnel, faintly lit by that silver glow from far ahead. She continued crawling. The tug on her ring told her that this was the way Paul had gone. She couldn't imagine he'd been very comfortable crawling through this—it was a tight fit for her, and he was a good six inches taller. At least the sides of the tunnel were smooth with nothing to catch on her sweater, which was up to her armpits now. She felt an extra pull on the yarn as she crawled and realized that her sleeves were now unattached, hanging loose on her arms, as the shoulders and neck of the sweater unraveled. She bit her lip and kept crawling.

Breann's hands and knees and back ached. The silver glow was getting brighter, but not any closer. She could feel her sweater unraveling the last few rounds of knitting around the collar. She put her hand to the yarn and held it, crawling with one hand only while she felt the stitches slip away between her fingers. As the last row fell apart, she stopped, leaning awkwardly on her elbow so she could use both hands. She tied the end of the unraveled yarn to the loose end of her left sleeve. When she was confident of the knot, she kept crawling, trying not to watch the sleeve twist around her arm as it grew shorter and shorter. When it reached her wrist, Breann paused again and attached it to the other sleeve. Her back was cramping horribly now, and she was sure her jeans were ripping. But the glow was brighter, almost an actual light.

When Breann emerged from the tunnel, she crouched where she was and stretched her back, blinking. The silvery light was much brighter here, coming from tiny lanterns that seemed to float at shoulder height, suspended in the air. A grassy lawn stretched away before her, cropped as neatly as a putting green. The grass shimmered with glistening dewdrops. A few small trees were dotted here and there around the edges of the lawn, casting strange stark shadows. She had emerged behind one of these. She stood slowly and took a step closer, staring. People were dancing around the grass, tiny people about the size of the Barbie dolls Breann had played with as a child, and in almost the same proportions. Their long legs carried them leaping and twirling around the ring, hand over hand as they passed each other. Their clothes would have suited a figure skater, Breann thought, all gauze and shimmer and not enough for the chill in the air, but perfect to flutter about them as they danced. They were so brightly colored that they dazzled, and for a minute she forgot why she was there.

Then there came a tug on her ring, and she blinked again and looked away from the dancers. Beyond them were other figures, small like the dancers and clad in similar attire, clustered around what almost looked like two thrones formed of twisted old tree roots. Breann caught her breath. The two people sitting in the thrones didn't need crowns to show that they were the king and queen. Their clothes shimmered brighter, somehow, and were made of finer gauze, and more layers of it. They had long robes that trailed over the seats of the thrones that seemed to have been woven of flower petals, probably mums since it was October.

Breann's ring tugged again. She looked up. Behind the thrones stood Paul. He looked so huge here that she should have seen him right away. But he stood half in the shadow of one of the trees, and his sage green sweater and black running pants made him look like part of the shadow too. He was watching the dancers with an odd half-smile on his face, and Breann wondered how long he'd been standing like that. How long would she have kept staring if the ring hadn't twitched her awake? She took a deep breath and stepped out onto the open lawn.

The dancing immediately stopped. Breann didn't remember hearing music, but the sudden silence echoed in her ears. Everyone stared at her, backing away to make a path as she treaded softly across the grass to the two thrones. Her blue sweater was no more than a narrow band at her wrist. When she reached the thrones, she bowed clumsily. Bowing wasn't something that was taught in American schools, but Gram's stories had always said how important it was to be polite—more than polite—to the fae.

"What is the meaning of this interruption of our revels?" The king's voice was reedy and annoyed.

"Your Majesties," Breann began, bowing again. "My husband is here in your company. I've come to bring him home."

"Have you indeed?" replied the queen. Her voice somehow reminded Breann of iridescent butterfly wings. Breann blinked, startled. "And have you brought anything in trade?"

Breann's heart sank. What could you give to the queen of the faeries in exchange for your husband? She couldn't remember if Gram's stories ever said. "What would you ask, Your Majesty?"

The queen studied her silently for a moment, and Breann was sure that she saw everything and then some. At length the queen said, "Winter is coming. Our people will be cold. You could knit us all sweaters in exchange. When all of the sweaters are finished, you may take him home with you."

"Sweaters?" Breann echoed faintly.

"Yes," the queen said. "We like green."

Breann understood then that the queen had seen quite a lot, including the fact that it was Paul's sweater that had led her to him. "May I sit with him while I knit?" Breann asked. "Since I'll be using the yarn from his sweater? I'd like it to keep him warm for as long as possible."

A tiny smile pulled at the corner of the queen's mouth. "How thoughtful."

"All right," Breann said. "I will knit sweaters for your people in exchange for my husband."

As she said it, she was fighting to remember if she'd left a set of double-pointed knitting needles in her notions pouch. She'd finished knitting one sock a couple of weeks ago but couldn't quite bring herself to start the second one, so she hadn't put the needles away. She just hoped she hadn't left the needles somewhere else around the house.

She bowed again to the tiny rulers, who no longer seemed interested in her. The music, if it was music, started again, and the silence now seemed less profound. Breann walked the few steps past the thrones to where Paul stood and stopped between him and the dancers, who were just beginning to move. He was looking around with the sleepy, dazed expression that he had some mornings when his routine was thrown off. He blinked at her stupidly, then his eyes seemed to come into focus.

"Bre?" he said. "Where are we? And why are we here?"

"We're in the Seelie Court," she muttered, slipping one arm out of a strap and swinging the backpack around so she could rummage through it. "Gram told me stories as a kid that I stopped believing years ago. I have to knit sweaters for them all before they'll let me take you home."

"You... what?"

"I'll explain later," she said. "Are you hungry?"

"Starving," he said.

She handed him a granola bar and a bottle of water, then pulled out her notions pouch. The double-pointed needles were there. "Thank goodness I'm disorganized," she breathed.

"What are you going to knit *with*, Bre?" Paul asked, watching her, more alert now that he was chewing solid human food.

"I'm going to have to unravel your sweater," she said. "I'll knit you a new one when we get home."

Breann sat on the ground beneath the tree. She took out the needles and did her best to guess at the gauge and stitch count for a figure the size of a Barbie doll—fortunately the sock she'd just finished used yarn that was a similar weight to the yarn of Paul's sweater. When she had a pretty good idea of what she was about to do, she took off her wedding band and felt for the knot. It came loose easily in her fingers. The yarn between her and Paul was instantly visible.

"What—?"

"I'll explain later," she said again.

She cast on quickly, following a simple raglan pattern she'd memorized. She adapted it as well as she could for the tiny size. It went quickly, and tiny sweater joined tiny sweater in the front pocket of her backpack. She didn't trust the fae enough to leave them lying around.

Paul sat beside her while she worked, obediently standing up and turning in circles now and then when she needed to unravel more yarn from his sweater. There were stretches of time when he zoned out again; she could hear his breathing slow under the effect of the fae magic, and his eyes stayed too fixed on one location. If she spoke or touched his arm he'd startle and respond. She kept her own eyes on her knitting, or on Paul. She didn't look at the dancers or at the faerie queen and king at all.

Time seemed to stand still while she knit. When she got too hungry to focus, she ate a granola bar and kept knitting. The silver light didn't change, and she didn't know if the night had passed, if it was only two o'clock in the morning, or if she'd already knit her way through another whole day. Her hands ached as if she had. Paul's sweater was up to his armpits, and then only the sleeves were left, like hers had been on the way here. At last she used the very last bit of the end of his second sleeve. The tiny sweaters filled the whole backpack. She stood up and stretched. Paul, with goosebumps on his arms, stood with her.

The dancers stopped again as they walked together, hand in hand, to the thrones. Breann tried not to notice that there seemed to be a lot more dancers now, a lot more tiny people staring at them. She hadn't counted the sweaters as she'd knit them. She and Paul bowed to the king and queen of the faeries. The king glanced at them and looked away. The queen looked up at her sharply.

"Have you finished?"

"I have, Your Majesty," Breann said.

"Then let us try them on," the queen said. She waved a hand.

One of her doll-like attendants stepped over to Breann, who took a tiny sweater out of the backpack and handed it down. The faerie slipped it on over her head. Breann had a moment of knitter's joy seeing that it fit perfectly, even if it looked odd over the faerie's ice skater dress. She only had a second to think this, though, before the next faerie stepped up to receive his sweater, then the next and the next. Before long, the backpack was empty. Breann looked at the gathered crowd of fae people. Her heart sank. Just over half of them had sweaters. She was fairly certain that this was more than had been in the dance when she had arrived, but not now.

"You have not clothed all my people," the queen said, a disdainful smirk pulling at her mouth. "I shall have to keep your husband after all."

This was what you wanted, Breann thought. *To destroy my connection to him and then keep him anyway.*

"Not yet," she said aloud. "I have no more green, but I can clothe the rest in lilac."

The queen frowned. "It will do."

Breann bowed and pulled Paul back to the tree. He'd gone vague and zoned out again in the presence of the king and queen and had missed the whole conversation.

"More knitting," Breann summed up. She was afraid of the power of words here.

It made her heart flop to begin the unraveling of her lilac sweater. This was her old favorite, and the one she'd worked the longest on. Every stitch that pulled out felt like a stab to the heart. But she looked at Paul, in and out of alertness as the half-sweatered dancers began their party again, and she knit on. She was going to get them home.

Her fingers were stiff and aching now, and she was cold. Her hands were slower and clumsier. But sweater after sweater went into the backpack. They'd finished all the granola bars, and were down to the last bottle of water. Breann's back and neck ached. She'd never knit a marathon like this before, and she promised herself she never would again. But at last she was done. She'd used the last of the lilac sweater. The only sweater left on either her or Paul was the few rows of blue stitches at Breann's wrist that miraculously hadn't unraveled with the twisting of the sweater beneath.

They returned to the thrones and again gave a sweater to each little faerie while the queen watched. The last two to receive sweaters were the king and queen themselves. Breann brought out her two remaining sweaters. The assistants took the robes from the monarchs' shoulders and put the sweaters over their heads, then draped the robes back around them. Though Breann thought they looked ridiculous, she held her breath, waiting.

The queen surveyed her people. The king, for once, seemed interested as well. Breann glanced over the crowd, all in sage green and lilac mini-raglans over their shimmering gauze, all watching the queen with wide, bright eyes.

"You have kept your end of the agreement," the queen said. "You may take your husband home."

"If you can find your way," the king added.

Breann ignored his jibe and bowed. "Thank you, Your Majesties."

She surreptitiously felt for the string that was attached to the remains of the blue sweater around her wrist and twisted her fingers in it. The backpack was on her back; Paul's hand was securely in hers. She felt the yarn pulling away across the close-cropped lawn, and she followed it. She wrapped the yarn around her fingers as she went, keeping the line taut so it would show the way clearly. The faeries in their tiny new sweaters parted to let them pass, but she ignored them. The eyes of the king and queen bored into her back. She ignored them too. All that mattered was the yarn that led her and Paul home. She found the entrance to the tunnel, completely hidden in dark tree-shadow. From this end it looked like two trees had leaned together until their trunks had merged, and below that merging point was the opening.

Breann pulled Paul down so that they were both on their hands and knees and made him crawl in first, then she crawled in behind him with one hand on the heel of his sneaker. It was awkward and even more uncomfortable this time around, but she didn't dare let go of him or take her eyes off him for a second, and she wanted to keep herself between him and the fae.

The crawl was as endless as the knitting had been, all uphill, and it got colder and colder the higher they crawled. At last there was a tight moment as Paul squeezed himself through the opening in the tree. Breann pulled herself through after him and found him standing, stretching his back and taking deep breaths of the early morning air. The sky was faintly gray above the trees. Fat snowflakes were falling between leafless branches, and there was already a dusting of snow in the open places.

Breann shivered. "Let's go." She didn't look behind her to see if the doorway in the tree had closed. In Gram's stories there was always a rule against looking back. She wanted to get Paul away before he looked too. She reached for his hand. He took hers and together they picked their way through the woods toward home.

When they reached the old logging road, Paul dug his cell phone out of his pocket. The time stamp read the very next morning. It had only been one night after all. "We're calling in sick," he said. Breann nodded.

The blue yarn led them all the way back to the side door of the house. Breann untied it and unlocked the door. She dropped the backpack just inside and cranked up the heat. After hot showers, they snuggled under blankets on the couch with mugs of hot tea and banana muffins. Breann told Paul everything that had happened that he didn't already know. He told her, too, what had happened the morning before when he'd gone running. He'd heard something beside the trail and stepped into the woods, not noticing until he was in the middle of it that there was a perfect ring of large mushrooms popping out of the undergrowth. Everything had gone black then, and he hadn't woken up until she'd gotten to the Seelie Court, and he still couldn't remember much of what happened after. Even as they spoke, Breann knew that they would never mention this again. Saying it aloud, here in the house, even between the two of them who had been there, felt unnatural.

But tomorrow she'd stop at the yarn shop on her way home. She'd begin his new sweater, and she would end it with a slipknot.

Unraveled

Korie frowned at the scarf in her hands. It was almost finished, but now as she looked at it, she saw all the mistakes she hadn't noticed. She hadn't noticed much of anything in the last two weeks since her sister's accident. Lara had loved this color, this yarn. Korie had been thinking of giving the finished scarf to her for Christmas. But Lara wouldn't need a Christmas present this year. Or any year.

Korie sighed and pulled the stitches off the needle, tugging on the yarn to unravel the stitches, row after row. She paused to wind it back around the ball. A noise in the kitchen made her look up; she was supposed to be alone in the house. But the voice was clearly Mom's—what was she doing home from work?—talking adamantly to someone from the insurance company. Korie had a moment of déjà vu. She'd overheard Mom having this same conversation a few days ago, almost word for word. Did insurance companies ever listen?

She tugged on the yarn again, unraveling several more rows. When she looked up, she found herself in the car outside the church, dressed for Lara's memorial service. Her heart began to pound loudly, frantically. This happened already. She wasn't about to do it again. Korie looked down at the yarn in her lap. She'd been knitting in the car up until the very last moment.

It was the only thing keeping her from a complete meltdown. Only now the stitches were not on the needles. The scarf lay loose on her lap, in the middle of being undone.

Undone. Had she somehow undone the past week? Had unraveling the scarf also unraveled her life? She slowly, cautiously, pulled the yarn again, just one row. She wound the yarn. She looked up.

She was back in her living room. She heard a car door. Her best friend Angie was making her way up the front walk with her overnight bag, coming over to stay the weekend. Korie didn't want to face her now. She pulled the yarn again. Several more rows unraveled. Korie stood looking into Lara's room, seeing everything scattered where Lara had left it, looking as if she'd be back any minute. Korie shut the door and pulled again. Her mom was on the phone, sobbing. Korie hadn't known who was calling or what they could possibly be saying that would make Mom so upset. She knew now, though, knew Mom would be coming in to tell her the news. Another pull of the yarn.

"Why on earth would you tell Mom?" Lara stood in the doorway, hands on hips.

Lara had come in hours after curfew the past two nights. Mom had questioned Korie about it. Korie hadn't meant to let it slip, but somehow Mom had gotten it out of her.

Lara was glaring at Korie. But instead of feeling her own temper rise, Korie just felt relieved to see her sister again. "I'm sorry," she said, her voice shaking slightly. "I couldn't help it. You know how Mom is."

"Don't blame her," Lara snapped. "It's how *you* are. You're a goody-two-shoes tattletale, and you always have been."

The unfairness of the accusation hurt as much this time

around as it had two weeks ago. How many times had Korie woken to see her sister sneak back home in the early hours of the morning and said nothing?

"Lara—" she said, unsure what to say next.

"Whatever. I'm going out."

"Don't take the car!" Korie pleaded.

"Why? Because Mom said I can't?"

Because you will take a turn too fast and hit a telephone pole. But Korie couldn't say that. Lara walked out and slammed the door.

Korie's heart hammered as fast as it had two weeks ago, but this time it was from fear, not anger. She looked down at the knitting in her lap. She'd hoped that she could stop her sister somehow. Maybe...

She slipped the stitches carefully back onto the needles and started knitting feverishly, the needles keeping tempo with the racing of her heart. She knit as the sun went down and her parents came home. There was homework in her backpack, she remembered. And if all went well, she'd need to turn it in tomorrow. But she wasn't expecting it to go well.

At seven o'clock, the phone rang. Korie's breath caught. Her mom picked up the phone. Her voice rose. Korie had already heard this a second time. She didn't need to listen a third. She pulled the stitches she'd just knit off her needles and ripped back.

"Why on earth would you tell Mom?" Lara scowled from the doorway.

"I'm sorry," Korie said again, her heart still racing. "I didn't mean..."

The conversation was going just as it had last time, which hadn't changed anything. She needed to do something different.

"Can we talk? Want to sit and watch *The Office* or something?"

Lara rolled her eyes in disgust. "I'm out of here." Korie heard the front door close behind her.

Had it been enough of a change? Korie slipped the stitches back onto the needles and began to knit again.

Seven o'clock. The phone rang.

Korie slipped the stitches off the needles before Mom even picked up the phone. She'd rip back farther this time, unravel back to before Mom questioned her. She'd go out. She'd lock her door and do homework with her headphones on. She'd stay over at Angie's house. Anything to avoid a conversation with her mother, who could read the answers even as Korie said something entirely different. She wasn't a tattletale. She hadn't actually said a word of the truth. But Mom knew.

If she didn't talk to Mom, would Mom still ground Lara for a week? Probably. Would she take away her car? Most likely. Would it change anything? There was only one way to find out. Korie grabbed the yarn and pulled.

Mermaid Calling

Let's get right to it: I don't believe my brother is dead.

I know my parents set up this appointment because they think there's something wrong with me. I should be grieving, right? Like they are. If I'm not on the verge of tears all the time I must be processing everything wrong, or holding it in in an unhealthy way.

But here's the thing: I *am* upset. I miss Jake. A lot.

I just don't think he's dead.

Why don't I think so? Well, that's a long story, but we have an hour to fill, right? First, you know the story of the little mermaid? I don't know if it's true—if it is, it happened a long, long time ago—but mermaids *are* real, and sometimes mermaid blood runs through ordinary people.

OK, that look means that you think I'm crazy, as well as in denial. But hear me out. Let me start again.

Did my parents say that Carina was Jake's girlfriend? Maybe. Probably. But the more important thing was that they were friends. They were—are—*best* friends. From, like, kindergarten, I think. Forever ago. They climbed trees and rode bikes together, worked on homework together. I'm pretty sure each of them only read half of the books for English class—any that Jake read, he'd tell Carina about, and she'd tell him about the ones she read. That way they both passed the tests.

Carina was my babysitter when she was old enough. Jake was the same age, so technically he could have babysat me, but Mom and Dad thought Carina was more responsible, I guess. She was already like a big sister—they're four years older than me, you know—and she was awesome. She'd bring over magazines she thought I'd like, and she'd team up with me to overrule Jake on what movie we'd watch. I feel a little bad for him now—he got stuck watching a lot of Disney princess movies for a while. I'm old enough now to not need a babysitter, but they'd still hang out at the house when they knew I'd be home alone, doing their homework at the kitchen table while I prefer to work on the living room couch.

I don't know when it all started. Not long after Carina started babysitting me, I guess. They were in middle school, and Jake was making new friends. He played soccer, and he hung out with some of the boys from the team. Most of the time Carina went too—she could be a tomboy with them just as easily as a girly girl with me. But there was this one time I remember: Jake had gone to the park with some of his friends from the team. Someone had built a tree fort, and the boys had staked a claim to it. Only thing is, there were no girls allowed. I don't know if there was an argument at the park or if Carina stormed silently off as soon as she was told she couldn't come in. Either way, there was a fight at our house that night. Mom and Dad were off at a school board meeting, so Carina was over. She gave Jake the cold shoulder for the first half of the movie—*Sleeping Beauty*—before he finally convinced her to talk about it. They went into the kitchen so they wouldn't ruin my movie, but I stood pressed against the door frame to listen. I was only seven, and I'd seen the movie dozens of times already.

"I don't like your new friends," Carina was saying. "Boys only? Really?"

"You're right, the tree fort rule was stupid," Jake said. "But most of the time they're not bad. They're pretty fun if you hang out with them."

"I'm not allowed to," Carina said. Her voice was colder than a freeze pop.

"So what do you want me to do?"

"Promise me you won't go anywhere I can't come. It's not fair."

Jake made that deal, on the understanding that it worked both ways—Carina wouldn't go where he couldn't either.

Not a big deal, right? Just a fight between friends, resolved, moved on.

But a week or two later they were both wearing these friendship bracelets—you know, the ones made of different colored yarn that's all knotted in a pattern? Everyone was making them for a while. But theirs were different. They matched, for one thing. And they weren't just stripes. The pattern seemed...I don't know. Like there was a meaning behind it, besides just, *we're friends*.

I asked Jake about it once. He tried to blow me off—I was just his annoying kid sister most of the time—but he admitted that it was a friendship bracelet with Carina. And he said they'd learned the pattern from an old lady at the park. She'd seen them making bracelets and called them over to tell them about the ones she'd learned to make from her grandmother back in eastern Europe somewhere. It sounded a bit weird to me, but Jake wouldn't tell me any more.

And then they got older and started looking at colleges. Jake was going to be an electrical engineer—my parents told you that, though, right? They've been telling everyone, like now he's going to miss out on the most exciting part of his life.

What? No, *I don't* think so. Frankly, I don't expect being a grown-up and having a job is all it's cracked up to be.

Anyway, they were looking at colleges, and for a while Carina was considering this all-girls school. They're rare now—inclusion is everything—but it had a really good reputation for sports nutrition, which she wanted to study, and their swim team was among the best in the world. It was right on the ocean too, so she could go surfing whenever she wanted. And that was Carina—always in the water whenever she didn't have to be in school, or when it wasn't so cold that the adults wouldn't let her. That's why their disappearance got so much press, you know? Two teens, who were both amazing swimmers, drowned at a calm, familiar beach, and no bodies found?

So Carina was looking at this all-girls school, and they were talking about it one night in the kitchen. Instead of homework, they were working on their application essays. I was taking a quick break from my own homework, and I was heading to the kitchen for a snack. I wasn't *trying* to overhear, but I kind of stopped in the doorway and stood there for a second before they realized I was there. Jake was twisting the bracelet on his wrist—those bracelets lasted for*ever*, or else he made new ones when the first ones broke—and he said something like, "What about our promise? Does that count anymore?"

Carina just stared at him. "It's not the only school I'm looking at," she said. "And I may not even get in."

Jake just made a face. Of course she would get in. She'd get into any school she applied to.

They saw me then, and I had to go to the cupboard. I grabbed the first box my hand fell on, which turned out to be marshmallow cereal—not a bad option, but not what I would have chosen for snack if I'd thought about it—and went back to the living room.

But it was weird, again. I admit, I started spying then. Not just accidentally overhearing things anymore, but actively following them and pressing my ear to doors and stuff. Not that I learned anything. Carina got accepted everywhere she applied, but she chose not to go to the all-girl college. She was going to go to another school with great programs and swim teams, which was located farther south, so that she'd be able to go to the beach throughout the school year. Their problem seemed to be solved. They were going to different schools, but they wouldn't be far from each other, and they would be able to visit.

The weirdest thing of all happened a week before they disappeared—did you know that they disappeared on Carina's eighteenth birthday? I wasn't spying on purpose this time. I was supposed to have a swimming lesson with Carina. She was at the beach before me, like she always was, already in the water. It was early on a Saturday, and the beach was empty. I was just passing the lifeguard's tower when I saw that Carina was standing in the water talking to someone. I hid in the shadow of the tower and watched them. The person she was talking to looked strange—hair that almost looked blue against the water but must have been black, pale skin as though she hadn't seen much sun lately. She stayed huddled down in the water so that it covered her shoulders, even though it barely came up to Carina's ribs. I couldn't hear what they said. And then, believe it or not, she ducked under the water and didn't come back up. But a fish—a surprisingly big one for being that close to the shore—splashed at the surface right near where she'd been. Carina seemed shaken and preoccupied when I crept from my hiding place for my lesson.

"We have to be careful of the tide today," was all she said when I asked her if something was wrong.

But something *was* wrong. Jake was bothered and irritable the next day, so I guessed she must have told him about it. They seemed to be having a lot of silent arguments when they were together, but they couldn't say anything out loud in front of me. I amped up my spying, of course, trying to find out more. Nothing came clear, though, until Carina's birthday. Jake was supposed to meet her at the beach to swim in the morning with a few other friends, and then she was coming back to our house for cake. Jake was up at dawn—way too early for him, and hearing him moving restlessly in the room next door woke me up. He didn't seem to be able to wait until eight to go to the beach. I got dressed and followed him when he left the house at six, peeking quickly at the note he left on the kitchen table. It only said: "went to the beach early. back later for cake."

I'd gotten pretty good at not being noticed by then, so I wasn't too far behind Jake when he crossed the beach parking lot and started to run across the sand. I started running too, but I was making for the racks of kayaks for rent. I crouched in the still-cold sand and peered out, nearly knocking one rack over when I saw them. Carina was standing in the water again, and the strange person was in front of her again—blue-black hair wet and gleaming in the morning sun, pale skin glowing. Jake was almost to them now. He'd kicked off his sandals and he was pushing through the shallow waves. Carina turned to look over her shoulder at him. I held my breath and strained to hear.

"I have to go," she said. "It's where I belong. It's in my blood.

I understand that now."

Jake shook his head. "Not without me."

"Jake—"

"We promised. You promised not to go anywhere I couldn't."

"But this is different."

"Is it? The only difference I see is that it's permanent."

The person who huddled low in the water in front of them said something that I couldn't hear. Jake held out his arm, and after looking at it a moment, the strange person turned to Carina. She held out her arm, too. It took me a minute to figure it out: it was the bracelets. They were showing her the friendship bracelets, that bound them closer than any ordinary friendship bracelet had the right to. The person said something else, and both Jake and Carina nodded. The person disappeared below the surface. Jake and Carina looked at each other, then dove after her. There were splashes where they'd gone under that were not like human feet kicking. They were more like the big-fish-splash I'd seen near Carina after she'd seen the water-person the first time.

And then they were gone.

I waited where I was for them to come back up, but they didn't. No heads bobbing up in deeper water. Nothing. I got up and went to where Jake's sandals still lay on the sand. I sat down and watched the waves and thought about what I'd seen. The world suddenly felt less real, and fairy tales felt more likely. I lost track of time, so I was still sitting there when the other friends arrived for the swimming part of the party. I don't know how coherent I was, but they got the idea that Jake and Carina were gone, and someone called the police.

And now you know everything I know. I've told it all to my parents and Carina's, and to the police. They all think I've made it up, fabricated a story as a coping mechanism. If they believed me, I wouldn't be here right now. But—do you read fairy tales? Do you remember any you read as a kid? Because really, if a girl had mermaid blood, wouldn't she spend all her time in the water like Carina did? And wouldn't the time for her to make a choice to live on land or under the sea be given at her eighteenth birthday? And I don't know where Jake got the power to put into those bracelets he made, but I think the water-person—the mermaid—recognized it and allowed him to come along because the connection was so strong. You see? So, no, I don't think they're dead at all. I think they're off swimming and exploring somewhere.

Together, just like always.

Knit Night

Aria flopped into the empty chair, tossing her project bag to the floor with a frustrated sigh. A couple members of the Knit Night crew raised an eyebrow before turning their attention back to their own handwork.

"What's up, buttercup?" asked Susan from beside her, taking a sip of a frothy latte.

"My invisibility cloak has a hole," Aria sulked.

"Darn it," Susan said.

"I know."

"No, I mean *darn* it, like darning, the mending technique."

"I know," Aria said again. "I've been watching tutorial videos all afternoon, and I just can't do it." She reached down to her project bag and pulled out a long piece of gray knit fabric which was definitely not invisible.

"No worries, sunshine, I'll show you. I had to learn a few years ago when the puppy got hold of an oven mitt and the heat resistance stopped working. Notions?"

Aria handed her the small zippered pouch. Susan dug through it for a yarn needle and some scissors. Aria pulled a ball of gray yarn from the bag and laid out the cloak so that the hole was on top. It was only about half an inch across, but any break in the fabric was enough to interrupt the flow of magic.

Susan cut a length of yarn and threaded it through the needle. She made a few slow passes, talking Aria through each step. "Your turn," she said, handing over the needle.

With gentle coaching, Aria managed, slowly, to repair the hole. She sewed the ends of the repair yarn under so they were hidden and snipped the last little bits off. The chatter around the table quieted as everyone watched the cloak. Almost imperceptibly at first, then more and more obviously, the cloak faded until there was no more than a faint haze, like the heat-shimmer over a fire, left where it had been. Everyone cheered, and a few raised their glasses. Aria hugged Susan, who winked at her. Aria sat back, feeling the invisible warmth of her cloak on her lap, and looked around the table. Tutorial videos were all well and good, but she didn't know how she'd ever survived without Knit Night.

Seventeen Cats

There were seventeen cats living in Larry's basement.

They had turned up out of nowhere, one at a time, over the past few months. There might have been more by now, but Larry had given up counting. He also had given up worrying about whether they had enough food. If they were hungry, they could go to someone else's basement. He didn't know how they'd gotten in. The ground-level basement windows were closed, but not particularly secure, so after the first two cats, Larry had gone to the hardware store and replaced them. The new windows were still tightly closed when he found the third cat, a gray tabby, circling his ankles as he threw a load of laundry into the washing machine.

Larry had stopped at the pet store on his way home from work that afternoon. He needed fish food, and he picked up a bag of cat food while he was there. He also put up signs at the pet store and around his neighborhood, hoping that someone would call to claim their missing cats.

But no one called, and another cat turned up two days later.

Larry was tired of buying cat food and tired of tripping over cats whenever he went downstairs to do laundry. He was tired of his clean clothes being covered in cat hair by the time he carried them upstairs from the dryer.

"Where are you coming from?" he asked the crowd in exasperation one Saturday morning. "Why are you *here?*"

One short-haired tuxedo cat stopped rubbing against his ankles and looked up at him with big golden eyes. "It's warm and dry," the cat said. "We like the sound of the washer. And the furrrniture is *very* comfortable."

Larry blinked down at the cat. The cat wasn't wrong—the couch and recliner were as old as the TV they faced, but that only made them conform better when you sat down. Larry himself had fallen asleep on both at one time or another, just as several cats were doing now.

But the cat shouldn't be right or wrong. The cat shouldn't have an opinion at all.

Larry hurried back up the stairs and slammed the basement door. He leaned against the kitchen counter and took a sip of lukewarm coffee from his cup. His hand was shaking. He had a talking cat in the basement. They might *all* be able to talk, but that was too much to think about.

When Larry had his breathing—and his trembling hands—under control, he decided to pay a visit to Mrs. Everly. He'd dropped by once before—somewhere around cat number five—to ask if she was missing any cats. She wasn't, and Larry assumed she'd stop by if any of hers did wander off. But this was getting ridiculous. If anyone would know what to do, it was the neighborhood cat lady.

Mrs. Everly lived in a small ranch house at the end of the street. Her lawn was always neatly kept, and her flower beds were brightly enjoying all of the rain they'd gotten this spring. Six cats were sprawling in the sun. Larry warily eyed the ones on the porch as he rang the doorbell.

"Good morning, Lawrence," Mrs. Everly said as she opened

the door and peered up at him through her big round spectacles. "You look bothered. Would you like to come in?"

"If you don't mind," Larry said. "I wasn't sure who else to go to."

He followed Mrs. Everly into the tiny living room. Three more cats were lying on the couch's floral slipcover. Another was draped over the back of a chair. Mrs. Everly ignored it and sat in the chair. The cat flowed over her shoulder and onto her lap. Larry perched uneasily on the edge of the couch.

"Now, Lawrence, what can I do for you?"

"Well…" Larry said. Now that he was here, he wasn't sure quite what he wanted to ask. "How many cats do you have?" That wasn't it, but it was something to pass the time until he thought of it.

"Twelve," Mrs. Everly said, smiling at the cats on the couch. "Elfred and Elton are asleep on my bed at the moment. This is Glenda." She gently stroked her lap cat between the ears.

Larry nodded. "I have seventeen," he said. "Maybe more. They're living in my basement, and I don't know where they've come from, and I don't know how to get them out. I don't want to call animal control," he added. "I don't think they'd believe me if I told them that the cats appeared out of nowhere and that the basement windows have been closed the whole time."

Mrs. Everly considered him thoughtfully. "Well, I can't take them, if that's what you were wondering."

"Not at all!" interjected Larry. "That's not—"

"Of course not." She rummaged in the basket beside her chair and came up with a ball of scarlet yarn. "Now, I don't know if this will work," she said, holding it out. "I learned this a long, long time ago from the cat lady at the end of *my* street, back before I had cats of my own."

Larry looked from the yarn to Mrs. Everly. "I know cats like yarn," he said when the pause had stretched on, "but would one ball really distract *seventeen* cats? And how would I get them up the stairs?"

"Don't be ridiculous, Lawrence. It's not for them to play with. It's to round them up. You roll the ball around the entire group, and when it comes back to you, you hold the ball and the end together to form one huge loop. Pull that loop up the stairs and out of the house, and as you do, you say a rhyme."

"A rhyme? What rhyme?"

"I'm not sure it matters," Mrs. Everly said. "It probably ought to say something about gathering the cats and about them leaving and not coming back."

Larry blinked at her.

"Well," she said stiffly, "if you don't want it, you can just call animal control. I have no other ideas for you."

"No!" Larry said quickly. "I'll try it." He reached out and took the ball of yarn. "Thank you."

"You're welcome," Mrs. Everly said. "And good luck."

As Larry walked home, he turned words over and over in his mind, trying to come up with a rhyme that said what he wanted it to. He wasn't a poet by any means, but by the time he opened the basement door and started down the stairs, he had something that he hoped would work.

The cats were stalking and sprawling and stretching and scratching everywhere. Larry got the last of the bag of cat food out and poured it into three bowls in the middle of the room. It worked. The cats rushed over to eat—in that unhurried, uninterested way cats have—so that nearly all of them were in the center of the room. Larry grasped the end of the yarn and rolled the ball. It bounced off the TV console and the closet door, turning the corners nicely. Larry was sure it would get caught in the corner by the washer and dryer, but a tuxedo cat—Larry thought it was the one that had talked to him, but he couldn't be sure—batted it back toward him before jumping up onto the washer. Larry lunged for the ball and caught it. He held the end, and the now much smaller ball, in one hand and began to walk backward up the stairs, saying his rhyme as he did.

"Gather cats and gather kittens
with the stuff you use for mittens.
Go outside and go away
and never come back, night or day."

The cats followed him. Some of them yowled and others looked grumpy, but Larry kept moving. There was a bit of a traffic jam at the back door, but they made it out. He led them all the way around the house and out to the street. It may have been enough to get them out of the house, but he wanted them off his property as well—to play it safe. When Larry and the whole string-full of cats were in the street, he let go of the end of the yarn and began to roll up the ball. The gathered cats put up their noses and stalked away, slinking off in all directions. Larry turned back to the house. A single cat sat at the end of the walk: a tuxedo cat with golden eyes.

"That was what you call a *glaring*," the cat said. "A glaring of cats."

Larry took a step closer. "Thank you for your help down there," he said. "That was you by the washer, wasn't it?"

The cat looked smug and twitched its tail.

"You weren't inside the loop then," Larry said.

"I wasn't," the cat said. "I'll go, if you ask nicely, but I'd rather stay. I like the couch, and I like riding the dryer, and you buy exactly my favorite kind of food. I promise that my staying won't bring any of the others back, and I won't be able to talk now that they've gone and taken the magic with them. "

Larry looked at the cat and sighed. "I suppose we could try it," he said.

The cat turned and began to prowl back to the house, then paused to look over its shoulder at Larry. "Aren't you coming?"

"Yes," Larry said. "In a minute. I need to return this." He held up the ball of scarlet yarn.

The cat slipped through the door, which swung shut behind it. Larry walked back down the street to Mrs. Everly's house.

"I'll have to go buy more cat food and litter," he muttered. "I suppose someday I'll be the cat man down the street for someone else." He frowned and promised himself not to let that happen. It was just one cat, after all. Just one.

The Spindle of Destiny

I've been at the winter sheepfold since before dawn, waiting. After the hard work of harvest, it's nice to sit with my back against the cliff rock in the autumn sun. I'm not worried—Dane will get here eventually. If the sheep do what they're told, they might make good time and get here today. If not, I'll sleep here tonight and be ready when he gets here tomorrow. We've done the same thing for the last four years. Before that Papa came to help Dane and to show me how it was done. And before *that*, Papa used to be the one bringing the sheep back from the summer pastures and Dane went to meet him. Back then I stayed home with Mama, arranging the harvest in the root cellar, spinning yarn for winter knitting, and wishing for more interesting work. Not that counting sheep is interesting. It isn't. But at least it's different, and it gets me away from Mama and the aunts.

I wake from my doze to bleating and the familiar purposeful yips of Dane's dog, Por. Dane named him Porridge as a puppy because his muzzle is gray, like he got into a pot of breakfast porridge and ate it all up. But mostly we call him Por. Dane is Por's favorite, obviously, but sometimes he listens to me too. I scramble to my feet just in time to see Dane and the first of the sheep, Por's head bobbing around behind and between them.

Dane grins as he sees me. "Right on time," he says.

"What are you talking about? I've been waiting all morning." I make a face at him and go to open the gate.

His grin widens. This is what we say every year. "Good to see you, Talya."

"I'd like to say the same," I say. "But you need a bath and a haircut. Maybe you'll be good to see tomorrow."

He laughs and whistles, and Por herds the sheep toward the gate. I let them in one by one, counting them as they come. By the time they've all been corralled and counted, fed and watered, it's dark. I'm glad to have Dane by my side as we start down the long path to the village, the wind at our backs, rustling the trees eerily overhead. Por's black fur blends into the darkness, only his white showing: his paws, the tip of his tail, and the white streak between his ears.

Halfway home, I freeze in the middle of the path. "I forgot my bag," I tell Dane.

I can't see my brother, but I know he's shrugging one shoulder like he always does. "You'll just have to go back tomorrow. It's too dark now."

I nod and fall into step beside him again. Moments later, Dane says, "Why does the sky look like that?"

We've come to a meadow, separated from the village fields by another band of woods. Above the trees the sky looks pale and yellow, though the stars are already coming out in the dark stretch behind us.

"Is a storm coming?" I ask.

"I've never seen it do that before a storm," Dane says.

We pick up our pace, rushing through the trees. Por trots beside Dane. The wind turns; I smell char and glimpse light through the trees. I guess what we will find: fire. Dane stops just behind the last of the trees. I stop too, staring. The stubble in the fields has been burned to black ash. The nearest orchard is in flames, along with the first few buildings of the village. I shiver.

Dane turns to me. "Stay here. I'm going to see what's going on."

"There's no cover," I say, glancing out again at the burnt fields.

"I have to try," he says. "There might have been an accident. They might need us."

The thoroughness of the burning doesn't seem accidental to me, but I nod anyway.

"If anything happens to me, take Por and hide out in the sheepfold," he says. He squeezes my shoulder and drops to the ground, crawling through the ash and soot away from me before I can speak.

Por sits beside me, watching Dane go. I rest my hand between Por's ears, grateful for the company. I lose sight of Dane before long. The soot on his clothes helps him blend with the shadows even better than he did before. I wait for long, breathless minutes.

Then suddenly Por slips out from under my hand and dashes away. He bounds across the fields after my brother. I hear a low cry from Dane and a sharp whispered command. A whine from Por. I hesitate, wanting to run to them but also wanting to obey Dane's instructions.

"What was that?" Loud men's voices shout. Torches flame to life. Firelight glitters off the metal they wear. I can't see Dane or Por from where I stand frozen at the edge of the trees. I picture my brother pressed flat against the ground, Por on his belly beside him, praying for the soot and darkness to hide them. But there are four men, and Por can't hide his white spots. The distant scuffle is over quickly. The men drag my brother and his dog away. The only light is the fire in the orchard. The only sound is the spit-crackle of flames.

There is nothing else for me to do. I turn, choking on the smoky air and my tears, and retrace our steps. The way feels much longer now, without even a dog for company. The sheep wake restlessly when I arrive at the fold, but they recognize me and sleep again, blissfully unaware of what has happened. I wrap myself in a spare blanket and huddle in a corner, letting the night-noises of the sheep lull me until my eyes close.

I wake at dawn and feed the sheep from some of the winter stores, then gather my things. I'm glad now that I packed extra food in case Dane was late; glad, too, of the blankets and other things kept here in case a shepherd gets snowed in with his sheep. Dane said to stay hidden with the sheep, but I can't. I know that whoever has attacked our village will sooner or later be hungry for meat, and there is an easy path leading to lamb chops. Not to mention that sitting hidden while horrible things happen to my family is the worst thing. I leave the sheepfold and begin to climb the rocky cliff.

I've climbed the rock face near the sheepfold dozens of times, beginning when I tagged along with Papa and got bored waiting for Dane. I know where all the best hand- and footholds are. It's harder with my satchel over my shoulder and a rolled-up blanket tucked like a scarf around my neck. I can't move as freely, and my balance is off. But I make it to the top. Here trees grow, and the slope is steep but not sheer. I pull myself upward, holding the trees for support. After an hour or two, I rest briefly, then move on. Most of the leaves have fallen, and I feel exposed, though it would take an eagle's eye to see me from our village.

The day goes on like this. When I get hot I unwrap the blanket from around my neck and tie it awkwardly around my waist like a second skirt. I don't know where I am climbing to, but I keep going. Wherever it is, I haven't reached it. The sun sinks on the other side of the valley, sending long red fingers of light between the peaks. Then it is gone, and I have only the fading light in the sky to see my way. I need to find a place to rest, someplace safe where wild animals won't find me. I see nothing but trees with branches too high to climb. Worry gnaws at me like hunger. I've rationed my food so that I will eat tonight and tomorrow morning, but that's it.

I look anxiously ahead. Suddenly, between the trees I see a light, like the candle Mama often places in the window to welcome weary travelers. For the first time I am a traveler, and I am so weary. I stumble in the dark and cling tightly to each tree as I pick my way toward the light.

It is indeed a candle in a window. The house is flush with the mountain side: a cave with a wall built across the entrance and a door and window cut into that wall. I knock, leaning against the doorframe to keep myself upright. Now that I've stopped moving, my legs feel like jelly and my stomach aches.

A shuffle of feet from inside and then the door opens. An old man peers out at me. His wild silver hair mingles with his bushy mustache and beard so that he looks like a dandelion gone to seed.

"What's this?" he murmurs, and his voice reminds me of a high wind through leaves. "A girl?"

"Please," I stammer. "Can you give me shelter tonight?"

"Of course, child, you're dead on your feet," he says. He steps back and motions for me to come inside. I stagger through the door, and he closes it behind me. The candle and a small fire in the hearth are the only light. The old man takes his candle from the windowsill and holds it up between us, studying me by its light. "You've come from the village down below, haven't you?"

I nod.

"What brings you up here?"

"The village," I begin, but I sway and he catches my arm and leads me to a cushion on the floor by the fire. He puts a bowl of apples and walnuts and oatbread on the floor in front of me.

"Eat," he says. "What happened at your village?"

"It was attacked," I say, shivering though the fire is warm. "They set fire to the fields and orchards. They captured my brother. I don't know about anyone else." I reach for a walnut, as much for something to do as to feed the ache inside me.

"I smelled smoke on the wind this morning." The old man sighs. "I knew she'd do something like this eventually, but she caught us off guard." He seems to be talking to himself not to me. "Not that we could have done much."

"Who?" I can't help asking.

"Which who?" he says. "The 'she' who did this or the 'we' who couldn't have stopped her?"

I blink in surprise. "Both."

"*She* is Kasmerra, the witch queen of the mountains."

"Who is she? Why did she attack our village?"

He sighs. His eyes are bright in the firelight. "Her story starts a long time ago. Eat," he says again, gesturing to the bowl. I bite into an apple as he looks into the heart of the fire.

"Kasmerra was one of four siblings born to a noble family. Each of the children showed signs of magical ability, and so each was trained according to their gift and inclination. The eldest loved the earth and all things that grew. The second

113

could see far, wide, and deep, and understand what he saw. The third loved the moon and stars and the motion of the night sky. But for Kasmerra no one thing was enough. She wanted every gift, to be best above all the others. So she studied in secret and learned of a way to take others' gifts for her own. She took the magic from her siblings and from her teacher and from anyone else with a gift she lacked. She continued to work in secret so that no one knew what she was doing until they had no power to stop her. What she is after now, I can't say. Perhaps there is an unknown gift in your village. Perhaps this is an attempt to stretch her kingdom beyond the mountain and control the valleys as well."

"But what can be done to stop her?" I ask.

"Not much," the old man says. "Eat and rest now. We will talk again in the morning." He shuffles slowly toward the back of the cave and into the shadows, as though his thoughts weigh him down with their heaviness.

I finish the food in my bowl in silence. I untie my blanket from around my waist and lay on the floor with my head on the cushion I've been sitting on. With my stomach content and my body exhausted, it takes me no time at all to fall asleep.

I wake in confusion, lying on an unfamiliar floor with an unfamiliar blanket. I blink up at the old man, able to see just the dandelion nimbus of his hair in the pale gray light coming through the one window. The past two days come back to me, and I sit up, groaning. My muscles ache from the climb and the cold floor.

"Good morning," the old man says. "Here is breakfast if you're hungry."

I am, and I gratefully accept the porridge he hands me.

"Do you know where you're going?" he asks as we eat.

114

"No," I say. Yesterday my goal was up the mountain and away, but I've done that.

"You might go farther up the mountain to see my brother," he suggests. "His house has a good view of the valley. You might learn more of your village from there."

I nod, and we finish our breakfast in silence. After eating, he hands me a wrapped bundle of food and a flask of water for my hike up the mountain. I slip it into my satchel and wrap my blanket around my neck, because the early morning air outside is cold.

As I leave, he says, "One more thing: the Spindle of Destiny." He hands me a small wooden spindle. It's no different than the ones we have at home, except that the whorl is carved with strange designs. It's a very strange parting gift to someone about to climb a mountain.

"What...? Why?"

The old man shrugs as if it's all unimportant, but his sharp eyes say otherwise. "It might come in handy," is all he says.

I blink at him for another moment, then put the spindle in my satchel and close the door behind me. I forget about the spindle after ten minutes of climbing. All my focus is on keeping my feet on the steep slope. I've been climbing for over an hour when I realize I don't know where this brother's house is—"up the mountain" covers a good deal of ground. All I can do is hope that whatever led me to the old man's house just in time will lead me to his brother's house too. Maybe it's Destiny, whose spindle is in my satchel. I roll my eyes and keep climbing.

After several more hours I remember that the old man never told me who is the "we" who were caught off guard by Kasmerra's attack and who couldn't have done much to stop her. I suppose he means himself and his brother. But I wonder who the old man is, to know as much as he does about the witch queen.

I have no energy to spare for more thoughts; the trees get sparser and more straggly as I climb higher. The sun is low over the distant mountains. The valley is already in shadow, but I'm high enough that pink-gold light still shows my way. I look eagerly, almost frantically, for any sign of the brother's house. I have very little food left and no way to start a fire. I know that as soon as I stop I will be cold, and it will get even colder with the sun down.

The very last rays of the setting sun gleam on the mountain above me. I look up, and I see it as clearly as if the sun were pointing a rosy finger just to show me: the glint of a window. A window in a house. I claw my way upward, using my hands as much as my feet. The trees by now can barely be called trees—they are no taller than I am, and as thin as one of my fingers—and I can't trust them to bear my weight. At last I heave myself up onto the final ledge. I sit there, panting. The house stands on the widest part of the ledge, built of stone and mortar so that it blends in with the rock. Once I've caught my breath, I stumble to the door.

It opens at my knock. The man frowning at me has streaks of white in his dark hair, and he has dark, hooded eyes. "Yes?" he says. "What do you want? I don't get visitors."

"Please," I say. "Your brother sent me."

"Karell sent you?" The man examines me closely. "Yes, I suppose he did. Come in, then."

He opens the door farther and ushers me inside, gesturing to a wooden chair at a tall wooden table. I sink onto it.

"Who are you? What's your story?" he asks, closing the door.

"Why did Karell send you?"

"My name is Talya. My village was attacked," I tell him. "They burned the fields and orchards, and they took my brother captive. Your brother said that you might have a better view to see what's going on."

The man frowned at me. "That's all he wanted? For you to get a better view?"

I shrug. "That's why he said to come see you. He also told me that a witch queen was behind the attack, and he gave me this." I pull the spindle out of my satchel. The man's eyes dart between me and the spindle. "He called it the Spindle of Destiny."

The man makes a face. "He always was dramatic."

He turns away to a cupboard and gets out a loaf of bread. My stomach rumbles loudly as I slip the spindle back into my satchel. I watch him slice the bread and ladle bowls of soup from a pot on the hearth. He passes me a bowl and a thick slice of bread and pulls a stool to the table to sit across from me.

"Your village wasn't the only one attacked," he says, after a spoonful of soup. "The whole valley is in ashes."

I stare at him, my spoon halfway to my mouth.

"I'll show you in the morning. Karell was right—I can see a lot from up here."

"But why would she...Kam...Kas..."

"Kasmerra."

"Why would Kasmerra burn the whole valley? I thought she wanted to rule it."

"That's an old theory, but it doesn't fit. Her armies have been moving through the valley toward the castle. The prince and his wizards haven't moved to stop her. They know who they're dealing with."

"They haven't? Why not?"

"I thought Karell told you about her. She'll take their magic before they get close enough to use it. That's what she's after."

"Oh."

We finish our dinner in silence. The man makes a bed for me on the floor by the hearth. With a brief word of goodnight, he disappears through a door. My mind is spinning, and I feel like I've somehow fallen into one of grandfather's tales. But my body is exhausted, and I fall asleep quickly.

Early sunlight streams through the window to wake me. I sit up to find the man seated at the table. "Eat some breakfast, then I'll show you the valley."

I nod and accept some of last night's bread with honey. When I finish, we both step outside onto the ledge. I can see now that he was right—my once-green valley is black and burnt. I'm thankful that at least the harvest is over and the fields were bare, but what has the army done to the stored food? And the homes? I can't see a single house standing.

"What happened to the people?" I am afraid to ask, but I have to know.

"I couldn't see," he says. "Some, I believe, are in hiding. Others may be rounded up in camps. Kasmerra will want hostages to use to threaten the prince."

I hope my parents and grandfather are in hiding. I don't know whether to hope Dane is in a camp or not. If he's a hostage, at least he's alive. For now.

"My sister lives up the mountain. She may have something you can do to help."

I want to protest that I can't fight an army or a witch queen. But I think of Dane in a camp, and I know I'll do whatever it takes.

"Take these." The man holds out a pair of knitting needles.

I reach for them automatically. "Karell would probably call them the Knitting Needles of Doom, but there you go. Tell her Koel sent you." He shrugs and walks back into his house. He closes the door behind him.

I frown after him, sliding the needles into my satchel next to the spindle. What a strange family.

I wrap my blanket around my shoulders and turn to the mountain. The slope is steeper here. I am studying it, trying to decide how to begin, when I notice the faintest hint of a path. I take a few steps onto it, keeping one hand on the rocks above. It is not easy, but it is better than scaling the rocks outright. The wind is icy up here with no trees to block it. My hands are soon numb, and I shiver despite the blanket I'm wearing around my shoulders. I slip and skid and scrape my knees on the rocks, but I press on.

The sun is high overhead when the path leads me to a cave. I can tell right away that someone lives here, but it is not as much like a house as Karell's cave. The entrance is plain stone, but there is a rock shaped into a comfortable seat for looking out. Farther in, I can see wooden walls and a door. I creep forward toward the door.

"Hello?" I call. I knock on the door.

"Who's there?" A woman's voice echoes through the stone cave.

"I'm Talya. Koel sent me."

The woman who opens the door is younger than her brothers, not much older than my mother. The gray in her hair is faint enough that I only catch glints of it in the sun. She blinks at me and opens the door for me to come in. "Too bright out there," she mutters. "Why did Koel send you?"

I take a deep breath. "The valley has been burned, including my village. He and Karell say a witch queen named—"

"Kasmerra," the woman sighs. "Of course." She leads the way farther into the room. I'm glad to see a fire, and I hold my hands out to it. "I'm Kassindra," she says. "Did Koel give you anything?"

"The Knitting Needles of Doom," I tell her, grinning in spite of myself. "And Karell gave me the Spindle of Destiny."

She rolls her eyes. "So now we're letting Karell name everything?" She goes to a cabinet and pulls out a little leather pouch. "Well then, here are the Pins of the Hero." She holds it out. I look at it, then at her. "Don't look at me like that. They may just save you sometime."

I take the pouch, if only to stop her glaring at me. "Koel said you might know something I can do to help my village."

"Not just your village, Talya." She bustles around the room, setting out cushions on the floor by the fire. "Rest now. You're going to have a late night."

I settle myself on the cushions, confused but glad to be warm. I doze off, waking only when Kassindra shakes my shoulder.

"Time to eat, then I'll show you where to go."

I sit up and take the dried fruit and meat that she hands me. When I finish, she gives me another packet of food, which I slip into my satchel.

"Come with me." She hands me a lantern then leads me through another door and into a series of caves. The first few look lived-in, the rest are just rough rock. At last she stops. "Keep going," she says. "Follow the caves and you'll reach Kasmerra. You'll know what to do when you find her. But I give you this warning: once you start, don't stop."

I nod, suddenly more frightened than I've ever been. Kassindra turns and walks back the way we came. I take a deep breath and continue on. The caves echo my footsteps. The lantern casts odd, moving shadows against the walls. I try to creep more quietly, darting my eyes this way and that. My heart is hammering so hard in my chest that I'm surprised the caves don't echo that too. Soon the caves close in and become a tunnel. Ever since leaving Kassindra's caves I have been walking uphill, but now the climb is steeper. At last it becomes so steep that someone has cut steps into the rock. The lantern doesn't show how far the steps climb. I am in a glowing bubble, unable to see more than a few yards ahead. The echoes press louder on my ears with the walls so close. I never thought I had a problem with underground, closed-in spaces—I've hidden in our root cellar often enough waiting for Dane to come find me. It was a game we played when Por was a puppy, seeing if he could sniff me out and then round me up and herd me to Dane. I pause, close my eyes, and think of my brother. My breathing calms; the panic subsides. I don't like this space, but I remember why I'm here. I open my eyes and press on.

Though the climb has felt like hours, it can't have been very long. My legs are tired but not weak, and I don't need a rest. The ceiling gets lower for the last few yards until the steps run right into it. I press my hand against the rock above me and find the handle of a trapdoor. I tug: nothing. I push, pressing against it with my shoulder, and slowly, heavily, it swings upward. I open it only a crack so I can peer out. This is a store room, full of crates and barrels and jars. I listen for long minutes but hear nothing but my own breathing and thundering heart. Very carefully, I ease the trapdoor up and open so that I can climb out. I creep around crates, keeping hidden until I reach the door. I am at the end of a short hallway.

A stairway leads upward. I tiptoe over to it and hesitate, my foot on the lowest step. A voice murmurs above, and a faint light reaches halfway down the stairs. I put down my lantern and begin to climb. The door at the top of the stairs is closed but not latched. I push it open enough to see into the room.

A tall woman in a long black dress stands at the far end of the room. Her attention is fixed on something I can't see, and she's muttering to herself or to whatever she's looking at. I can't make out the words, but they don't sound happy or kind. The light in the room comes from candles on the walls, and they glint on the woman's hair, which flows like a river down her back and pools on the floor behind her. The stone floor is so dark that I can't tell where the hair ends and floor begins. I'll have to be careful when I go in to do...whatever it is I'm going to do.

Kassindra said I'll know what to do when I get here, but I'm clueless. I look around the room for anything that will tell me how to defeat Kasmerra. What I have brought with me feels useless: a bit of food, a lantern, and tools for working with wool. Kassindra knew I was going to face the witch queen. Couldn't she have given me something more useful than *pins*? I cast my eyes around the room again.

A strange gleam on the floor catches my eye. I study it, not because I think it will help me but because it is distracting. It is like dark water reflecting light, like the way Kasmerra's hair catches the candle glow. But it is halfway across the room from where Kasmerra is standing. No one has hair that long. The more I look, however, the more convinced I am. Her hair not only falls to the floor behind her—it fills the whole room.

And suddenly I know what to do. I push open the door a bit more, just enough to reach in my hand and gently lift a lock of ebony hair. I take the spindle from my satchel. There is enough hair here that I could spin for several minutes before Kasmerra feels the slightest tug. Taking a deep breath, I begin to spin.

I've never spun human hair before, but it isn't hard. I spin and spin, expecting any moment for Kasmerra to stop her muttering and turn around, or to cry in pain and put a hand to her head where the hair pulls. She doesn't, though, and I keep spinning. The lake of hair covering the floor doesn't seem to be shrinking at all, even though I spin for hours. I pause to stretch my hands and back, then spin more.

When dawn light peeks through the windows, I can see that I've already cleared half of the floor. My stomach aches, and I pause for a second to reach into my satchel for the food Kassindra gave me. The pouch of pins meets my hand first and I take it out and put it on the stair beside me, digging deeper for the dried snacks. I pull out a strip of dried meat and chew it slowly, my hands returning to their work.

I've just swallowed my second strip of meat when a shriek freezes my blood. I look into the room to see Kasmerra striding toward the stairs where I'm hiding. Her eyes flash as she throws open the door.

"Who are you? What are—No!"

Her eyes are fixed on the spindle in my hands. I give it another twist.

She points at me, her fingernails long and claw-like. She screeches words that I don't know, and suddenly I'm knocked back against the wall by a concussive force, like a battering ram against a gate that just barely holds. I keep my grip on the spindle, and I hear Kassindra's voice in my mind: *Once you start, don't stop.* My hands shake as I give the spindle another spin.

Kasmerra's face whitens, making her blazing dark eyes even more terrifying. More pointing, more words, another concussive force that pushes me back into the wall. But I keep spinning, and now I can see the confusion and fear in her face. She throws another spell at me, but I'm ready for it now, and I don't stop spinning.

She glares at me. "They've protected you," she snarls. "But they can't guard you from everything." She lunges at me, her talons reaching straight for my eyes. I fumble for my satchel, for my pocket knife, for anything to defend myself with. My hand falls on the pouch of pins. I grab one and jab it into her wrist as I turn my face away from her clawing fingers. She screams and stumbles backward into the room, tripping and falling on her own hair.

I start spinning again, faster now. *Once you start, don't stop.* I only hear a couple of low moans from Kasmerra before she falls silent, and I don't look up. I keep spinning until my hand reaches for more hair and comes up empty. The spindle stills. I look up into the room.

It is completely empty. No Kasmerra. No hair. Just sunlight on stone floor.

I take a deep breath. *Once you start, don't stop.* Time for the Knitting Needles of Doom.

I smile as I take them out. Can you take Knitting Needles of Doom seriously, even if you're using them to defeat a witch queen? I cast on directly from the spindle and start knitting. There's no pattern for trapping a witch queen, so I just knit and knit. I make a mistake, but instead of going back and fixing it, I make the same wrong stitch again and again until it becomes a design. I keep knitting, letting my hands knit whatever they want, letting the design form itself from what the needles and yarn choose. I reach the end of the spindle and bind off.

It is a long rectangle. Shawl-sized. The quantities make my head spin, but the sun is going down and I've barely eaten anything and I haven't slept since yesterday afternoon. So maybe there's nothing wrong with a roomful of hair plus a witch only filling up one spindle and then somehow making a whole shawl. I don't stop to think about it. *Don't stop.* I grab the pouch of pins. I ought to have wood to pin the shawl to, and water to wet it, but there is none. Shaking my head at my own ridiculousness, I step into the room and lay the shawl flat on the stone floor. Knowing full well that a metal pin won't push into stone, I try anyway. And it works. The point of the pin sinks into the stone and stays there. My breath catches, and I stare at it for a moment before I hear Kassindra's voice in my head again: *Don't stop.*

I push in another pin, and another, until I've pinned the whole shawl. Except that there's a gap in one edge with no pins. I look around to see if I've dropped one, and I see it: the pin I stuck into Kasmerra's arm as she reached to claw out my eyes. It lays on the stone floor a couple feet away, having fallen from her as she was spun up. There is a smear of her blood on the side of the pin, but I don't wipe it off. I could only use my dress to wipe it off, and I don't want her blood on me. I just stab the pin through the gap in the shawl and into the stone floor.

"Nice touch," says a voice behind me.

I turn where I'm kneeling. Kassindra is smiling at me. Behind her, Koel and Karell are coming through the door that I'd hidden behind.

"Thank you," Karell says, his white hair as wild and dande-liony as before.

"It worked," I say.

"Yes," Kassindra says. "She will remain trapped here until the stone wears away and the pins fall out."

"She said…" My thoughts are slow and confused. "She said you protected me."

"We did." Karell smiles. "We gave you food and shelter when you would have starved or been eaten by wolves."

"But her spells…"

"Couldn't touch you because that protection clung to you. We couldn't do much, but with a little protection from all three of us, it was enough."

"I still don't understand why she…did what she did." I gesture vaguely, including the valley, the army, the past, everything.

Kassindra shrugged with a sad smile. "Kassie always wanted to be the best. I suppose it comes of being the youngest."

Kassie… "Then you're her sister and brothers, the older siblings she stole magic from."

They all nod. The men's faces are stone-cold, but Kassindra's still holds a trace of sadness.

We all look at each other for a long time. Finally, I stand up. "If she's—" I gesture to the shawl—"then will her army…?"

Koel steps forward. "I can show you." He puts his hands on either side of my face. "Close your eyes."

I close them, trying to keep my breathing slow and even, though I'm nervous of what I'm about to see. Gradually, in my mind's eye, I see the valley spread out before me, soaring on eagle-wings toward my village. I descend in large spirals over the village, and I see clearly the blackened remains of the fields and the orchards, and the dirty brown streak that used to be a clear, silvery stream. My stomach twists, and I whimper, but Koel's hands hold my head still. Closer and closer I get to the village, and then I see them: big men in metal coats, with weapons in their hands. They stand guard outside a new enclosure with rough wooden boards for walls. Suddenly behind them a section crashes outward, and people I know—my brother, my neighbors, my father's friends—pour out, swinging fire pokers and farm tools. The soldiers drop their weapons and raise their hands, and Dane whistles Por forward to herd them into the enclosure as neighbors bearing the right tools secure the wall again.

The vision fades, and I blink up into Koel's face.

"Is it true?" I breathe.

He nods. "It has just happened."

"How did I see it?"

"I am the brother with a gift for vision," he shrugs. "You saw so clearly because it is easier to share a vision with someone who has a gift of their own."

I gape stupidly at him.

"Don't look so surprised," he says. "You've just spun up a sorceress and knit her into a shawl. Not everyone can do that." He walks back to the door, pausing with his hand on the frame. "And you did it without training." He disappears down the stairs.

"He's right," Kassindra says. "Sometimes a gift lies dormant until its bearer is in great need. I can't train you to use your particular gift since I don't have the same one, but I can teach you what I know."

Karell has been watching me closely this whole time, studying my reactions. He says, "Sindie, the poor girl is tired. This is a lot to take in." He smiles gently at me. "Go home. When you're ready, I will teach you the beginning. Then we will decide who you'll learn from next."

"First, though," Kassindra puts in, "come rest at my house and eat. You'll fall down the mountain if you try to climb down just now."

I nod weakly. Rest and food. I follow them to the stairs, picking up my satchel from where I dropped it. The spindle and knitting needles are piled next to it.

"Keep them," Kassindra says. "They are your destiny and your doom, since you've proven yourself to be the hero."

I put them into the satchel and sling it over my shoulder, too numb to do anything else. I pull the door shut without looking behind me.

I wake at dawn before Kassindra's fire, and though my body wants to sleep for hours longer, I get up, wrap my blanket around my shoulders against the chill wind, and start down the mountain. I lose my footing on the stony slope and slide a good distance, scraping my hands and shins but making the descent in half the time it took to climb. I pass Koel's house and the treeline, glad to use the trees to keep from falling. But there are still places where I slip on the fallen leaves and skid a ways before I catch a trunk and stop myself. I trip and slide right past Karell's cave house. I reach the cliff above the sheepfold right as the daylight fades, descending as carefully as I can in the dark and dropping the last few feet.

The sheep greet me with distress as I creep, exhausted and bruised and a little bloody, into the fold. I realize with a guilty lurch that no one has fed or watered them in the whole time I've been away. I fetch water and hay and grain for them, and I clean myself up as well as I can in the dark. Once the sheep have food, they stop paying attention to me, so I wrap myself up in my blanket and fall asleep.

I wake to a familiar voice. "Talya?" Dane is sihouetted against the early morning sun, peering into the sheepfold from the cave mouth.

I stand up, laughing in relief. "You're alive!" Not that I doubted Koel's vision, but I prefer to see things with my eyes, up close.

"So are you!" He pushes his way through the sheep and hugs me. "What happened to your hands?"

I look down at the bandages I wrapped hastily around my scraped palms last night. "I slipped on some rocks," I say. "It's fine."

"Are the sheep as exciting as you expected?"

Of course he thinks I stayed in the fold like he told me to do. I let him keep thinking that. "Not even a little."

We feed and water the sheep together and start back toward the village, Por trotting beside Dane as if the last few days never happened. I'm willing to pretend they didn't. And someday, when the village is rebuilt and thriving again, maybe I'll remember those few days, and maybe I'll climb the mountain again.

The Spinning Wheel

Sarah bought herself the spinning wheel for Christmas, along with a bag of fluffy white-and-gray wool roving.

"I knew it," laughed her friend Mandy. "Knitting's the gateway drug. It's all downhill from here."

Sarah had learned to knit five years before, from Mandy. She'd been going crazy in the first few months at home with a new baby. Mandy already had a spinning wheel, a loom, and a collection of knitting needles and crochet hooks that would make a craft store jealous.

Sarah had laughed at Mandy's "gateway drug" joke. She loved knitting, but she had no extra time or attention for other hobbies and she didn't expect to for a while. Two years after baby Ella came baby Liam, and babies—and toddlers—are a lot of work.

But the two little ones had kept growing, becoming a little more independent, able to put their plates in the sink and get their own water from the fridge. They could go potty on their own and wash their hands.

Then came school.

Sarah didn't know what she would have done without her knitting needles on Ella's first day of kindergarten. It was nothing like her first half-day of preschool, which had, quite frankly, been a welcome relief for Sarah. To only haul one kid along to the grocery store was wonderful. She and Liam had even gone for walks when the weather was nice. But kindergarten? A whole day without her little bumblebee, not knowing whether Ella was eating her lunch or making friends. Sarah knit half a sweater that first day, her needles mirroring the anxious rhythm of her heart.

Ella had loved her first day of school, and each day after that got progressively easier.

And then Liam started preschool.

It was nice, at first, being able to go to the gym or run errands alone. But Sarah was surprised that, more and more now, she was bored. Even knitting more difficult patterns wasn't enough. So when Mandy had mentioned in passing that a friend of hers was selling a used spinning wheel, she'd jumped at the chance. She bought it for herself but allowed her husband, John, to wrap it up for Christmas, since, even used, it wasn't cheap.

Mandy had come over to help her set it up and show her how to use it, and other than a few emergency video chats, Sarah was off to the races. She loved it—loved the rhythm of the treadle and the whirring of the wheel, loved the pull and twist of the wool between her fingers. She was so proud of her first bobbin that she immediately texted Mandy a picture. And her second bobbin was no less amazing, because then she was able to ply them together. Into *yarn*.

Mandy came over to show her how to wash and air dry her new yarn, and together they picked a pattern for Sarah to knit with it: a simple hat to show off the eccentric beauty of that first lumpy handspun. Sarah spun more wool and knit more hats for the whole family, and gradually her lumps smoothed out a bit.

She also ran out of wool.

She bought more, but good wool wasn't cheap, unless she bought it as a fleece and did all the work to turn it into clean roving herself. And despite her boredom, she didn't have *that* much free time. She asked Mandy for suggestions.

"You can spin other things," Mandy said. "Alpaca, obviously. Angora is from rabbits, and mohair is from goats. They're more expensive, but even some dogs and cats have fur long enough to spin."

Sarah was a little weirded out by the idea of spinning cat hair at first, but as time went on and she ran out of wool again, she decided to try it. Their long-haired cat, Butterball, hadn't been particularly thrilled by the arrival of children and the decrease in attention she got afterward. So she submitted willingly enough when Sarah lured her onto her lap with treats and began to brush her. One brushing didn't give Sarah nearly enough to work with, but she repeated the process every couple of days until Butterball would jump onto her lap at the sight of the brush, even without treats, and Sarah had a gallon plastic bag full of cat hair.

Mandy showed her how to card it with wool so that it wouldn't be quite as hard to spin, and soon she had more yarn, all with a beautiful golden sheen. Ella insisted that Butterball's first yarn was for her, so Sarah spun more and knit her a sweater.

"You can't wear it to school," she told her daughter the first morning, when Ella was beginning to pull it over her head. "Some kids are allergic to cats. You can wear it when you get home."

That afternoon Ella put on the sweater as soon as she kicked off her shoes. When Sarah had finished hanging up coats and going through Ella's backpack for school papers, she found Ella curled up on the couch with Butterball in the sunny spot near the window, dozing.

"Must have been a long day," Sarah murmured, tiptoeing past.

After her success with Butterball's fur, Sarah was on the lookout for other long-haired pets. A friend down the street promised to save all the fur she brushed from her German shepherd mix. A coworker of Mandy's raised goats, and some of them had longer hair. "It's not mohair," Mandy said when she delivered the bag of fiber, "but give it a try."

Sarah did. She knit a hat for John with the goat yarn, which turned out to be very soft. And the German shepherd/wool blend became a sweater for Liam. He loved it and insisted on wearing it on the way to school. Sarah didn't have the heart to tell him no, but he had to put it in his backpack until it was time to come home.

Sarah was feeling rather proud of herself. Her yarn was more and more consistent, and she was adapting easily to using different fibers. And it made her heart soar when her family *chose* to wear the things she made them.

Until she started noticing things.

John, who drove for a postal carrier and delivered locally during the day, usually packed his lunch and ate whatever she made at dinner time. But there were days now when he would stop to pick up fast food in addition to finishing the lunch he'd brought, or he would eat two peanut butter sandwiches when he got home before dinner was ready. "I don't know," John said when Sarah asked him about it. "Some days I just feel like I'm hungry all the time and want to eat everything I can get my hands on."

Then Liam got into trouble at preschool.

Sarah called Mandy that afternoon. "Something's wrong with my family," she said as soon as her friend picked up.

"Um, hi, and what do you mean?" Mandy asked.

"They're just acting...strange. Like Ella—she seems sleepy every day when she comes home from school. I thought it was just that she loved having a sweater made of Butterball's fur, so she was snuggling up with the cat more. But the other night she wasn't interested in video chatting with my parents, which is not like her. Usually she's shouting and twirling and bouncing off the walls."

"You're right," Mandy said. "I've never seen her with less than 120% enthusiasm. Is she getting sick?"

"She doesn't have a fever," Sarah said, peeking in at her daughter, who was again curled up with Butterball in the sunny spot on the couch. Liam was building a puzzle on the floor next to them. Sarah paced away down the hall. "And then—get this—Liam pushed another kid at preschool today."

"What? Not sweet little Liam!"

"I know! It was so weird. I was dropping him off, and we saw his friend Toby hanging up his backpack. Another kid said it looked like a baby backpack and took it from the hook and pretended to be a baby. I was about to step in when Liam just rushed up and pushed him!"

"Oh my goodness," Mandy said.

"Yeah, we had to talk to his teacher, and I took away his TV time for the week. I was so embarrassed. What has gotten into my family? Why is my angel boy suddenly all protective?"

Sarah stepped into her bedroom and pushed the door mostly closed behind her so that the kids wouldn't hear. Her gaze fell on the little brown and black sweater that she'd just hand-washed and laid out to dry on a towel on her bed. Her stomach plummeted.

"Mandy," she said. Her voice had gone up three octaves. "Can you come over please?"

Sarah hung up and started cooking dinner while she waited, shooting uneasy glances at the bedroom and the family room, where Ella was still lounging in her Butterball sweater, watching her brother build his puzzle.

When Mandy knocked, Sarah yanked the door open and dragged her friend by the wrist down the hall.

"What's up?" Mandy asked as she trotted after Sarah. "Now *you're* acting weird."

"You have no idea," Sarah muttered. She stopped just inside the bedroom door and gestured at the bed.

"I don't get it," Mandy said after a long pause.

"It's the yarn," Sarah said. She was almost afraid to say it out loud. "Liam was wearing a sweater made with German shepherd fur, and he acted like a German shepherd defending his friend."

Mandy looked skeptical.

"Ella's favorite sweater is made with cat fur," Sarah went on, "and she's barely left the couch all week."

"OK…" Mandy said, still unconvinced.

"John's been wearing the hat made from the goat hair you brought me," Sarah said. "He's been eating everything in sight."

Mandy looked from Sarah to the sweater on the bed. "So your family is taking on the personalities of the animals whose fiber their clothes are made from?" She took a step back and leaned against the door frame.

"There's something wrong with that spinning wheel," Sarah whispered, tears pricking at the corners of her eyes.

"OK, hold your horses." Mandy put a hand on Sarah's arm. "Before you go out and burn the spinning wheel, let me call my friend Teresa and see if she noticed anything weird when she used it."

Sarah nodded and wiped her eyes. Mandy left to get dinner for her own family. Later that night, she called Sarah.

"Teresa didn't notice anything," Mandy said. "But she always used sheep's wool."

"So her family were acting like sheep?" Sarah guessed with a weak smile.

"Maybe," Mandy said. "But sheep's wool seems to be fairly safe. And I was thinking—there are plant fibers you can spin. Cotton and linen wouldn't change anyone's behavior."

"I guess," Sarah said, her heart lifting. She really did love that little wheel. "I saw something online the other day about someone taking little scraps of yarn and spinning it into their wool. Bits of recycled acrylic yarn wouldn't hurt anybody, right?"

"Exactly."

Sarah looked at the pile of handspun hats and sweaters she'd gathered from around the house. She tucked them into a vacuum seal bag and pressed all the air out, then stashed them at the back of the top closet shelf. Then she picked up her knitting needles and a skein of store-bought acrylic yarn. It would be a little while before she could get her hands on some plant fibers. Maybe she could grow flax in the garden next summer. In the meantime, Ella would want a new sweater.

Goose Brothers

My stepmother is a witch.

I mean that both literally and figuratively. Not only does she practice magic, she practices bad magic.

She also hates me.

Not just me—my brothers too. She hates all four of us. I still don't know why she married our dad if she doesn't like kids. Her eyes get all hard and cold when she looks at us, and sometimes there's a little twitch at the corner of her mouth, like she's amusing herself by imagining all the awful things she could do to us.

Of course, we didn't know about the witch part when they got married. We just knew we didn't trust her.

The twins were weirded out, but they're eighteen (their birthday was in September, just before the wedding), so if it all went south, they could move out. Stephen and I aren't so lucky. Stephen's fifteen, and I'll be fourteen next month.

"It'll be ok, Em," Stephen told me, when I confided my worries to him. "Owen and Michael will take us in if we have to run away."

I made a face at him. I was being serious, and he was teasing his little sister. Besides, it's not like I *want* to leave Dad. He's awesome, if a little clueless and sometimes at work too much.

We've been in the habit of getting ourselves up and ready for school without a grownup for years, pretty much since Mom died. Evelyn mostly leaves us to it, but sometimes she wanders in while we're eating breakfast. She pours herself a cup of coffee, glares at us, and disappears back upstairs.

This morning I finish my breakfast before she comes down for coffee. I leave the boys still discussing the football team's chances (the twins are on the team—Stephen plays baseball) and hurry back to my room to get my backpack together. Last night I was doing homework until the moment my head hit the pillow, so my books are still scattered across my floor.

I can hear her voice when I come back down. That's enough to make me hesitate outside the kitchen door—she never talks to us if she can help it. The door is open just a crack. I can't see anyone's faces from here, but I can hear her clearly.

"You were supposed to take out the trash," she says. "And *you* were supposed to load the dishwasher." I can picture her turning her glare from my brothers to the sink, which I know is piled with dishes.

"We were at practice!" Owen protests.

"Your father has let you get out of hand and make excuses." Her voice has a dangerous edge. "I won't tolerate it."

I bite my lip.

"If practice is what's causing you to shirk responsibility," she says, "then you won't be playing football anymore. Or much else, I think."

There's an odd rustling, as though of feathers, but I can't figure out why. Then she laughs, and I hear the squeak of the French doors opening.

"Go on, off with you."

I crack the door open farther so I can see around the frame

and see the tail-ends of three huge birds being shooed through the glass doors. Birds? Had someone left a door or window open and they'd wandered in? But how? And from where? And hadn't I heard Evelyn open the door?

The truth hits me, and I turn and sprint down the hall to the front door, wrenching it open and slamming it shut behind me. Three huge Canada geese are circling over the house. They each swoop low over me before they fly away, toward the reservoir on the far side of town. I suppose if I were a goose I would go there too.

What am I thinking?

My watch beeps at me, and I start speedwalking toward school. It's a good thing I have my backpack already slung over my shoulder—there's no way I'm going back inside.

The twins usually drive us in their beat-up Honda Civic, dropping me off in front of the middle school before continuing down the street to the high school. I've never walked to school by myself before. Not that I *can't*, of course, but it feels weird. Everything feels weird right now.

My brothers are geese. My stepmother is a witch.

I stumble through the school day in a daze, not even hearing my name when I'm called on in Spanish. Laci, my best friend since kindergarten, pokes me in the ribs. I sputter a nonsense response, and the teacher asks if I'm feeling OK. I'm not, but I nod anyway. She doesn't believe me, and she calls on someone else instead.

Laci knows I'm not OK. She asks me what's going on every time she runs into me at my locker, especially after I walk right by on the way to the cafeteria without seeing her.

I can't tell her. There's no way she'd believe me, for one thing. For another, I don't want to say the words out loud. Like maybe if I don't say anything, I'll go home and my brothers are all in bed with the flu or something. I shake her off by telling her I think *I* may have the flu.

I walk home alone.

The house is silent when I close the door behind me. A sudden idea pops into my head—Evelyn is still at work. Witches have spell books, right? I take the stairs two at a time and drop my backpack inside my bedroom door. I look down the hall to the open door of the room my dad and Evelyn share. I tiptoe across the hardwood floor, even though I know there's no one home and I'm being ridiculous. A small bookshelf serves as a bedside table. I crouch in front of it and begin to scan the titles.

"You won't find anything interesting there."

My breath catches in my chest. I turn slowly to where she's standing in the doorway.

"Unless you're looking for *Pride and Prejudice.*"

I can't decide if I'm more scared or angry. I go with angry, because that feels better than petrified. "You know what I'm looking for."

"A way to bring your brothers back?" she sneers. "How cute. You think you can break the spell?"

I'm sure as heck going to try. I turn back to the books.

"I already told you, you won't find it there. But, you know…" She comes over and sits behind me on the bed. "Watching you struggle might be fun. I'll tell you how to break it."

She has my undivided attention. "First, you can't tell anyone what you are doing or why, or say a word about what happened to your brothers. If you do, they'll be stuck that way forever." Her smirk grows. "You need to get wool—raw, unspun wool—and make sweaters for them. You have exactly six

140

months. If you do it, they'll be turned back into boys. If you don't, they will not." She shrugs.

I glare at her and get to my feet. I want to say so many awful things, but I am my brothers' only hope, and I can't risk joining them as a goose. I turn and storm from the room.

"Where are you going?" she calls after me.

"YouTube," I snarl.

Her crow of laughter chases me down the hall.

I don't have a laptop or phone of my own yet. Dad says I'll get a phone when I start high school and high school sports. Arguing hasn't changed his mind, but Stephen, who just got his own phone last summer, will usually let me borrow his if I ask. I go to his room now instead of my own. His backpack is on his desk chair, packed and ready to go. The room suddenly feels cold and creepy, which it never has before. I grab the backpack and take it back to my room. His phone is in the front pocket. I kick off my shoes and sit cross-legged in the middle of my bed, searching for videos.

I watch until my stomach reminds me how long it's been since lunch. I put the phone down and fall back onto my pillows. What kind of ridiculously antiquated skill is spinning? Do people still do that anymore? (If YouTube is any indicator, yes. But I never thought that would be me.) I take a deep breath. Wool isn't so bad. She could have said I need something impossible to get, like freshly brushed fur from an angora rabbit (yes, I've stumbled across a video for those too). Or something impossible to work with, like stinging nettles or poison ivy. What's the kid's name who lives on that farm out past the reservoir? We used to give him a ride home after baseball practice sometimes. I sit up and grab Stephen's phone again. They might still be on the same team. I scroll through his contacts, looking for a name that rings a bell. There: Jeremy Stills. I send him a message—*hey, this is Stephen's sister Emma. Do you have sheep? I need raw wool for a project I'm working on*—then slip the phone into my pocket.

Evelyn is not in the kitchen when I sneak downstairs. It looks like she's had more coffee, but the plates in the sink look the same as they did this morning. I open the dishwasher and start loading it, wishing Owen and Michael had done their chores last night and knowing it wouldn't have made a difference if they had. I start the dishwasher running then make myself a sandwich, using a paper towel as a plate so that I don't make any more dirty dishes. I take my sandwich and a can of soda upstairs to my room. I don't usually drink soda on school nights—that's a house rule, and my brothers make sure I don't break it even when Dad's working late—but they're not here, and I need the caffeine so that I can stay awake and watch more videos.

I trip on my backpack just inside my room and decide I should do my homework before I pull out Stephen's phone again. I sit at my desk with my books piled up, realizing that I'm not sure if what I wrote down in my planner is accurate at all. I could call Laci, but she'd ask more questions, and I can't risk that, not now that I know for sure what talking could do. I muddle my way through it, then watch videos in bed until I fall asleep.

The next morning, I wake to a message from Jeremy: *sure thing. I'll drop it off on my way to school.*

I throw my things into my backpack, slipping Stephen's phone into the front pocket. I eat breakfast quickly and wash my bowl, keeping my bag close at hand in case Evelyn comes in and I need to make a quick exit. I hear her moving around upstairs just as a knock comes on the front door.

"Got it!" I holler. *Please stay upstairs*, I think as I rush to the door and pull it open.

Jeremy stands outside, holding two big trash bags full of whitish fluff. He grins at me. "I didn't know how much you needed."

I smile back. I like his grin. He's cuter than I remember, with his ruffled mousy brown hair and green eyes that crinkle. "That's great, thanks."

I reach for a bag, and he steps inside to help me carry the other one up to my room. "You home alone this morning?"

"My stepmother is here," I say.

"No brothers?"

"No," I say, my heart suddenly racing. "They're...away."

"Oh," he says, looking like he wants to ask more, then shrugging. "Want a ride to school, then?"

"Um, sure, thanks."

He leads the way down the walk to a battered green Ford. I expect to see his mom or someone in the car, but he goes around to the driver's seat.

"You're sixteen?"

"As of last week," he says. He turns on the radio and hums along to the cheerful pop song that crackles out of the speakers. It's only about two minutes to the middle school. He pulls over and I climb out, thanking him for the ride and the wool. He grins again and waves before pulling away.

Laci is waiting for me outside the front doors. "Did you just get a ride from Jeremy Stills?" she asks.

"Yeah," I say. "He's a friend of Stephen's."

"He's *cute*," she says.

I nod and turn to the door, but she stops me with a hand

to my arm. "Are you going to tell me why you were so weird yesterday?"

"I told you, I wasn't feeling good."

"Uh-*huh*." With the raised eyebrows, that's Laci for *I'm not buying it.*

"It's complicated. I've got a lot on my mind."

"Which we share with friends who can help us," she prods.

No one can help me. "Not this," I say, and I walk into the school.

The rest of the school week is awful. Of course I have written down the wrong pages of math problems to do, so I have none of the right answers. I try to pay more attention, but it all suddenly feels like a giant waste of time. My brothers are geese, and I have six months to spin enough yarn for three sweaters, not to mention learn how to knit them.

I hurry home and pull out Stephen's cell phone as soon as I'm safely in my room. The videos I've watched show that you can spin with a spinning wheel (way faster) or a drop spindle. I have no way to get a spinning wheel, but a drop spindle looks simple enough to make. I find some instructions for a DIY spindle (really not that hard, it turns out). With an old CD (it's all scratched up, but even if it wasn't, who listens to CDs anymore?) and a giant novelty pencil that Laci brought back from her trip to Washington, DC, I head out to the garage where Dad's fix-it stuff is. I dig through his tools to find the hot glue gun. Dad has fixed a zillion toys and helped make dozens of Halloween costumes with this. Fortunately there's still a glue stick in it. The pencil is a little too small for the hole in the CD, but the glue fills the gap easily. I dig a little hook out of Dad's case of odds and ends. It's from a set used on Michael's bulletin board. I get a little twist in my gut as I remember the day they hung up that bulletin board. I twist the hook into the end of the pencil and hurry back upstairs to start spinning.

I don't care what anyone says, spinning is *hard*. The videos make it look so easy, but you have to keep the spindle (a.k.a. pencil and CD) spinning, and you have to keep feeding it wool, *and* you have to make sure it's more or less consistent and not ridiculously lumpy. *AND* when you get distracted by the wool and forget the spindle, it'll completely untwist itself, so you have to spin it all over again. No wonder Evelyn thought this would be funny. I'm ready to throw it down in tears, but I won't let her win, so I keep spinning.

This is my life now: school all day, where half the time my homework's wrong because I'm not paying any attention to it, then spinning all evening (and usually in the morning before school). I eat cereal or sandwiches or leftover takeout that Dad puts in the fridge. He's been working late every night this week. Usually this would bother me, but I'm actually relieved because I don't know what I will say to him when he notices the boys are gone. I'm honestly not sure if he's noticed yet—he's gone before I get up, and he's home after I fall asleep (sometimes still in my clothes with the spindle in my hands). He probably thinks they've had a string of late practices.

On Saturday morning, he pokes his head into my room. I'm just waking up, and I'm glad I put away the wool and spindle in my closet before I fell asleep last night.

"Morning, Em," he says. "I promised Evelyn I'd repair those shelves in the bathroom today, so I'm headed to the hardware store. Anything you need?"

I shake my head.

"Evelyn said the boys are on a sports trip this weekend. Know anything about it?"

I shrug. I'm angry with her for lying to my dad, but I'm glad I don't have to come up with a cover story. "I guess she signed the permission slips," I say. "There wasn't a lot of advance notice."

"No," Dad says. "Well, I'll be back in a bit. Love you."

"Love you too." I watch him close the door of my room. What are we going to tell him next weekend, and the one after that? I feel sick. I hate lying to Dad, but if I ever want my brothers back, I can't tell him the truth.

After another week it's a little easier to fake normality at school. I write down the correct assignments, and I pay attention. I get my homework done before I leave school so that I don't have to waste spinning time. Laci rolls her eyes the first couple of days I spend the whole lunch period doing math, but soon she gets bored and starts sitting with other girls in our class. I don't mind. I need to concentrate, but I feel guilty for blowing her off.

The next weekend, Dad knocks on my door. I drop the spindle into the drawer of my nightstand and shove it closed as he opens the door. "When did you last see the boys?" he asks.

"Last week," I say, choking back a lump in my throat.

He frowns. "Why didn't you tell me they didn't come back from their sports trip last weekend?"

My stomach knots. "I—nobody told me how long the trip was for."

"I called the school on Wednesday," Dad says, coming to sit on my bed beside me. "There was no sports trip."

I blink at him, unable to hide my alarm. Fortunately, Dad thinks I'm alarmed that my brothers are missing, not that the lie is blown and there's no way to cover it. "I'm calling all their friends before I call the police—do you know where Stephen's phone is?"

I grab it from my nightstand and hand it over. "He let me borrow it," I explain.

"Did he say where he was going?"

I shake my head. "He didn't say anything. I—I don't know if he expected to go anywhere." It's the truth, as much as I can manage.

Dad nods heavily and sighs. "Your birthday is next week. Are you planning your usual sleepover with Laci?"

I've almost forgotten my birthday is so soon. Sleepovers with Laci are always a time of sharing secrets and talking about everything, but I have a huge secret she can't know. "I don't really feel like it this year," I say. "Maybe just cupcakes from the Sweet Shop."

He nods again and gives me a one-armed hug before leaving the room.

By the next weekend, I can't spin. I can't stay in my room another minute. It's sunny and warm, and the perfect day to play soccer or Wiffle ball in the back yard. I suddenly miss the boys so badly it hurts. I swipe Stephen's phone from where Dad left it on the kitchen counter, then wheel my bike out of the shed and take off across town. I'm pretty sure Dad wouldn't let me ride all the way to the reservoir by myself, but he got called into work this morning (he peeked in to apologize and tell me that he'll be home with birthday cupcakes tonight), and Evelyn hasn't said a word to me since *that day*, so there's no one to tell me not to. I'm pretty sure Evelyn wouldn't mind if I had a bike accident.

It's a lot farther to the reservoir than I thought, and I have to push my bike up the last hill, but I get there. I lay my bike down in the grass. Holding my breath, I walk slowly toward the large group of birds by the water's edge. At least half of them are ducks, but there are several Canada geese there too. Will I be able to tell my brothers from the other geese? Will they recognize me? I let out my breath in a squeak of alarm as three geese peel away from the crowd and charge toward me, honking. Have you ever been charged by a goose? Not fun. I stand my ground, even though I'd rather be running, and they slow down. They keep honking at me, though. When they're close enough, they rub around my legs like housecats. I suppose that's the closest geese can come to hugging. I drop to the ground and put my arms around the nearest. He nips gently at my ear. I let him go and hug the other two. I can't tell who's who, but it doesn't matter right now.

I spend the next few hours sitting on the ground with my goose brothers around me. I remembered to grab the bread bag, so I pull it out of my bike basket. There are only a handful of pieces left, but my brothers seem to appreciate it. I rip up and throw a couple of pieces to the ducks and other geese to keep them from coming after me. I eat a granola bar myself. My brothers eye it but don't try to take it.

I ride home and put my bike back in the shed as the sky starts turning pink. Dad is pulling into the driveway, and I see that, in addition to half a dozen specialty cupcakes, he has takeout bags again. I miss taco night, when Michael cooks, or spaghetti made by Owen. (Stephen makes a perfect bagel with cream cheese, but that's hardly cooking.) Maybe I should try cooking—I've helped the boys a zillion times—but I don't want to waste the time.

He takes the food into the kitchen. I run upstairs to get changed. He didn't notice how sweaty I was from the long ride, or the goose feather stuck to my jeans, but no need to push it. Evelyn is with Dad in the kitchen by the time I come back down. They stop talking as soon as I push the door open. Evelyn glares at me, but hides it with her coffee mug when Dad turns in her direction.

"Happy birthday, sweetheart," Dad says lightly. "I hope you don't mind Chinese."

"Perfect," I say. I'm getting better at lying. I fill a plate with lo mein and sweet and sour chicken. I grab an egg roll and take my plate to the table. I don't want to stay in the same room with Evelyn, but I know Dad won't let me eat in my room, especially my birthday. I take a huge bite of egg roll. I'm starving, so it's no trouble to keep my mouth too full to speak. I'm afraid of saying something that Evelyn will use against me. They're both tense from the unfinished conversation. I put my plate in the dishwasher, grab a cupcake, and eat it in two bites. It's lemon-with-lemon-filling, but I barely taste it. I slip out the door and back upstairs, not sticking around to listen as I hear them start talking again.

I text Jeremy for more wool later that week. When he brings it by the next morning, I ask how much I owe him.

"Don't worry about it," he says.

"I'm not going to be finished this project for a while," I tell him. "I'm going to need a lot more. I'm sure you can't just keep giving it to me. Don't your parents sell it?"

He shrugs awkwardly. "It's usually fifteen dollars a bag, but for Stephen's sister, I'm sure they'll take ten."

I nod and hand over a twenty dollar bill. It's all the cash I have without asking Dad to take me to the bank. Jeremy pockets it, shrugs, and offers me a ride to school. Laci is walking up the path to the school with two other girls as I get out of the car.

She raises her eyebrows at me. I give her a half smile and wave. She turns and laughs at something one of the other girls says.

The next weekend I ride out to the reservoir again. "I'm going to fix this," I tell my three geese. "I'm working on it. But I just spent all my money on supplies, and I don't know how to get more."

One of the geese honks, nuzzles at his own chest by bending his neck in half, and then stretches his neck out toward me and honks again. He stares hard at me. I'm mystified, and it must show on my face. He does it again, and again. The other two start doing it too.

"Umm," I say, "you want me to scratch your tummy?" Isn't that a dog thing?

He shakes his head and honks again.

"I was talking about money, and you did that—" He did it again. "So... are you saying you have money?" He nods. "You have no pockets," I point out. "I don't think you have any pennies hiding in those feathers."

He nips at my wrist and glares at me.

"Oh, am I being stupid? Well, speaking *goose* is new to me." I sigh and hug my knees. One of the other two comes over and rests his head on my arm. "You were saying the same thing, weren't you?" I ask him. He nods. "You all have money. You mean I should go through your stuff and find your wallets?"

All three geese nod emphatically, honking louder than ever.

"That's stealing," I protest, but it's really not, if they're giving me permission. And the money is being used to bring them back.

So when I get home, I rummage around their rooms and return to my own room with three wallets. Now I'm able to pay Jeremy the next time he brings me wool.

"How much more do you need?" Jeremy asks as he gives me another ride to school. "You must be making a huge project."

"Kind of," I say. "I don't know. I might have enough now." I have a laundry basket in my closet full of dense, lumpy balls of yarn, each with a bobby pin securing the loose end so that it doesn't all come untwisted. I've never made a sweater before, so I have no idea how much I'll need.

"What are you making?"

"It's a secret," I say. "I want to surprise everyone."

That night I start watching knitting videos and searching for sweater patterns. My head is ready to explode by the time I fall into bed. I think I can get the hang of knitting—I'll have to skip my visit to the reservoir this weekend so I can ride into town and buy needles—but sweaters are complicated. All of the patterns include special stitches for shaping the shoulders and the neck. I don't have time to learn all that. But honestly, I think, as I lay awake looking at the ceiling in the dark, a sweater's pretty much two squares sewn together plus a couple of rectangles for the arms. Right? Hugely simplified, of course, but I'm not going for fashion, here. I just need them to be approximately sweater shaped. That decided, I fall asleep.

Knitting is harder than it looks, too, it turns out. But I keep at it with my new needles, and after a few days I feel comfortable enough beginning one of the sweaters. Each day I watch my progress grow, knit stitch after knit stitch. I empty my backpack that weekend and fill it up with yarn and my needles so I can work on it at the reservoir while my brothers keep me company. I wear a sweatshirt and throw a warm hat in the backpack—riding over will warm me up, but then I'll be sitting and knitting.

But when I get to the reservoir, the geese are gone. I look

all over for them before realizing that geese fly south for the winter. My chest goes all tight. I wish I had been able to say goodbye before they left. The ducks are still there, and they come over looking for bread. I wonder how much longer they'll be there. I give them all the bread I have and begin to ride home.

I haven't gone far when a car pulls off to the side of the road ahead of me. I recognize the beat-up green Ford immediately. Jeremy opens his door halfway and leans his head out.

"What are you doing all the way out here?" he asks.

"I rode to the reservoir," I say. "I like it there." I liked it better when my brothers were there.

"Isn't it getting too cold for bike rides?"

"A little," I admit.

"Let me drive you home," he offers.

I want to be alone, but I'm still tired from the ride here, so I accept. He helps me load my bike into the trunk. I can feel him shooting me concerned looks from the driver's seat as he takes us back through town, but I keep my eyes fixed out the window. I really don't want to answer any questions right now.

He parks in front of the house. Neither car is in the driveway. His frown deepens. "Your parents aren't home?"

I shrug. "Dad'll be home later. I don't really keep tabs on my stepmother. She was there when I left."

He's silent for a long moment. I'm about to get out, but I can tell he wants to say something. "Have you seen Stephen recently? Or Owen or Michael?"

I bite my lip. I last rode to the reservoir two weekends ago, which isn't exactly recent. "No." And I won't get to see them again until spring. Tears well up. I push open my door and go around the car, wiping my eyes on my sleeve and hoping he doesn't see. He meets me at the back of the car and opens the trunk. We wrangle the bike out in silence, but he hesitates before he leaves.

"You going to be OK in there?"

I know he means with no parents at home, but I think he also means with no brothers. I nod. "I'm fine. Thanks for the ride."

He nods and gets back into the car. I push my bike around the house to the shed as he drives away. With no one home, I grab a snack and hide out in the twins' room. It feels just as creepily empty as Stephen's did, but they have a TV and DVD player, and I need a distraction. I grab the first disc that comes to hand—*Christmas Vacation*—and press play, knitting through the whole movie, and another, and another.

When Dad comes home, he finds me there. I've made several inches of progress, and I'm rather proud of myself. I didn't hear him come into the house, so I don't hide my needles in time. He comes in and sits on Owen's bed beside me. "What are you working on?"

"Home Skills," I invent quickly. "We have to learn some kind of old-fashioned skill—you know, sewing or knitting or weaving or whatever."

Dad looks from me to my needles and puts his arm around me. "Well, you're doing a great job. Are you hungry?"

I suddenly realize I am. We both stand up, and I see Dad look around the room with a sad frown.

Ever since my birthday Dad has been coming home earlier from work so that he's home for dinner. We still eat a lot of takeout—Dad's never been much of a cook, and Evelyn's not the homemaker type (what did Dad see in her, anyway?)—but we eat it together. Dad always looks preoccupied, and he's getting frown lines on his forehead. As weeks pass, I notice Dad and Evelyn are stopping more conversations the moment I enter the room. One time I overhear Dad say that he was called in to his boss's office because his work performance has been suffering. They wanted him to work overtime to make up for it, but Dad said no. It makes my heart leap a little, that Dad would choose to be home with me. But I worry about him, too. He's dealing with a lot—the boys missing, fights with Evelyn, and pressure at work. If I could just finish these sweaters soon, I could at least solve one of the problems, probably two.

I stay up later to knit than I probably should, and I set my alarm a little earlier. I'm getting faster, too, as I get more used to the rhythm of it. I finish two squares and two rectangles, then two more squares.

Winter passes without me noticing. I don't go sledding even once or have a single snowball fight. I spend all of my free time in the twins' room, watching old movies and knitting. Two more rectangles, two more squares.

Then one day, I hear a sound that stops my heart. HONK! HONK HONK HONK! I'm walking home from school, and I freeze in the middle of the sidewalk and look up. A big V of noisy geese flaps high overhead. I race home. Dad's already there, so I can't sneak off to the reservoir. But I set an early alarm for Saturday morning. Dad's still been going in to work a couple of Saturdays a month, and lucky for me, this is one of them. I'm off on my bike as soon as his car is around the corner, a bag of bread and my knitting in my backpack.

I'm breathing hard by the time I push my bike up the last hill. I've been sitting around too much all winter. But I forget about my aching legs and red-hot face when I see the geese by the water, and my three special geese run toward me. I drop to my knees and hug them all. I ask them where they went for the winter, what it was like, what did they eat. I don't expect an answer. "I missed you," I tell them, and they all nod and honk loudly.

I pull out my knitting, and they gather around, tilting their heads to examine it. "Only one more piece after this," I say.

The next morning I wake up so stiff that I can barely get out of bed. I should have stretched after riding for the first time. Dad's already downstairs when I inch my way downstairs for breakfast. I yawn (it starts out just for show but becomes very real very quickly) and hope that my slow shuffle across the kitchen will be mistaken for sleepiness. Dad just passes me a bowl and a box of cereal.

I ride out again the next weekend, and this time I remember to stretch when I get there. I'm just getting off my bike at home when a car slows down on the street beside me. I look up, alarmed—Dad shouldn't be home yet. But it's Jeremy. I lay my bike on the still-brown grass and jog over to his open passenger window.

"Warm enough for riding again?"

I shrug. "Once I get going."

"You still have all the wool you need?"

I still have a couple of balls in the basket. "I think I'm good," I say.

"Just let me know if you need more." He grins, waves, and drives away.

I pick up my bike and wheel it to the shed, and I wonder for a second why Jeremy was driving down our street. It's not like he has to pass through on the way into town. Was he checking to see if Stephen is home yet? But he'd know that from school. Was he checking on *me*?

The next week I get called into the guidance counselor's office at lunchtime on Wednesday. I've only ever been in here once, last year, to fix my schedule. I sit awkwardly in the chair by the secretary's desk until I'm called in. Miss Ainsley smiles at me from the behind her desk.

"How are you, Emma?" she asks in that way grown-ups have. It's not a question, it's an assumption that you're not OK, and they want you to dish.

"I'm fine," I say. "Thanks. How are you?"

"I'm well," she says. "How are things at home?"

You wouldn't believe me if I told you. "OK," I say.

"I know your brothers are—hmm…" She watches me with a mix of concern and pity on her face. "Is there anything you'd like to talk about?"

"I'd like to go to lunch, actually." I cringe at how rude the words come out, but it's the truth, and it's the only truth I want to say right now.

Miss Ainsley sighs. "All right, Emma. But if you ever do want to talk, my door is always open."

I nod and leave.

I visit my goose brothers that weekend and show them my progress on the final sleeve. Not that they can tell it's a sleeve. "I'll be able to start sewing them together soon," I tell them. By the following weekend I've finished it. I want to stay home and sew, but I need to see them, too. "We're almost at the deadline," I tell them. "I don't know if talking to you counts against me, so I won't say much, but I should have everything finished soon. If I leave water out for you, can you come to the house? I want you close." I'll fill up the old kiddie pool from the shed that nobody every got rid of and leave it in the back yard.

They nuzzle up against me with quiet, loving honks. I don't

tell them that we only have three more days. I've set reminders on Stephen's phone every month, and this last month they've been every week. If I don't have the sweaters on the geese by Tuesday, this has all been a waste of time.

I find another YouTube video on how to sew knit pieces together. It looks easy enough, so I get to work, using a bent-up paper clip as a needle since I don't own one and don't have time to buy one. It works, although my progress might be faster with a real needle. I sew the sides of two squares together, leaving a gap at the top to fit the sleeves in, then fold two rectangles in half and sew them into tubes. Attaching the tubes to the squares is the trickiest part, and both end up crooked. The whole thing ends up totally wonky, but at least it's recognizable as a sweater. I move on to the next one.

By Monday morning, I have two sweaters done and the third half done. I've sewn the square sides and one of the arm tubes. I can't bear to leave them home—what if Evelyn did something to them as soon as I left?—so I stuff them into my backpack. I pull out the half finished one at lunch, opting to sew instead of do homework. I'm glad now that Laci and the others have made a habit of leaving me alone, because I can't explain what I'm doing, and they'd be sure to ask. The first sleeve is attached. One more to go.

Miss Ainsley finds me in the cafeteria a few minutes before the bell rings to go to class. She looks worried as she surveys me. I shove the final sleeve back into my backpack. "Mr. Willson wants to see you," she says finally. "I was heading this direction, so I told him I'd send you over."

"Oh." I blink at her. Why would the principal want to see me? I haven't done anything, have I? "OK. Thanks."

I sling my backpack over my shoulder and trudge through

the halls to the principal's office. The secretary smiles kindly at me and tells me to have a seat. I sit and pull out the sleeve again. As long as I'm waiting, I might as well be working. I don't like the way my hand shakes as it pulls the paperclip through the stitches.

I wait for several minutes, giving my full attention to the wool in my hands. A familiar voice startles me into looking up. "Dad?"

He smiles and comes to sit beside me. "How'd you end up here, sweetheart?"

"I have no idea," I plead. "Why did they call you?"

He shrugs. "She didn't say."

I put the sleeve away—I can't work on it in front of Dad—and just then, the principal's office door opens. "Emma," Mr. Willson says. "Mr. Findlay. Come in, both of you."

We stand up together and follow Mr. Willson into his office. There are two chairs facing his desk, surprisingly comfortable ones, and I sink into the one farthest from the door. There's a breeze from the open window. It chills me and reminds me I only have two more days.

"I called you both in today," begins Mr. Willson, "because some concerns have been raised about Emma. For one thing, we're worried that she's home alone too much."

Did Jeremy say something? He's the only one who would have noticed. "I'm not," I protest. "Evelyn's home in the morning before school, and Dad's home for dinner."

Dad looks at me. "It's been a difficult time," he admits. "After my sons…. The kids always looked after each other, and now we're finding a new normal. Is that what this is about?"

"Not only that," Mr. Willson says. "Miss Ainsley has noticed that Emma has been distant from her friends, and she's concerned that Emma may not be eating or sleeping properly."

Dad gives me another look, and this time I feel like he's seeing me fresh. I haven't been sleeping as much as I used to, and my meals are haphazard at best. I often skip breakfast or forget lunch, or just grab a handful of crackers or a granola bar. But Dad doesn't look any better. I don't think he's been sleeping well, and I doubt he has more than coffee before he eats dinner with us. "I don't think any of us have been taking care of ourselves properly in the past few months," he says quietly. "We'll work on that. But, Em, is it true that you've pulled away from your friends? What about Laci?"

I blush.

"Why?" Dad asks.

"I couldn't talk about it," I say carefully, "and she didn't understand."

"Miss Ainsley seemed to think there was something to do with the knitting you've been doing so feverishly."

When had she noticed *that*? I only started taking the knitting to school in the last few weeks, and I still focused on homework first.

"That's a Home Skills project, right, Em?"

Before I can nod, Mr. Willson says, "Emma isn't in Home Skills this semester."

"Did you not turn it in on time?" Dad asks me.

I open my mouth but nothing comes out.

"It's not for Home Skills, is it?" Dad says. I shake my head weakly. "What is it, Em? What are you making?"

I can't tell them. I can't. I'm so close.

Dad reaches across and pulls my backpack from my numb fingers. He unzips it and pulls out the half-finished sweater first, then the two finished ones. He lays them on the desk.

"What is all this?" His voice is gentle, but I know he won't let it drop until he gets an answer. "I won't let you have this back until you tell me the truth." I stare from Dad to Mr. Willson, who looks confused. I doubt he expected a couple of lumpy sweaters to be the sticking point in the conversation.

A honk sounds outside the window. Then another, and another. My heart leaps. Before I know what I'm doing, before Dad can reach out and stop me, I'm on my feet. I scoop the sweaters off Mr. Willson's desk and dump them through the open window. I press my face against the glass, peering down to see the ground outside, but I can't see directly below. I hear a rustle of feathers from outside and the scraping of chair legs behind me.

Dad is by my side, his hand on my shoulder, trying to turn me to face him. "Why did you do that?" he demands. "Why won't you just tell me what's going on?"

But now I can't turn away from the window. "Look," I whisper.

There on the grass below sprawl three teenaged boys. Their jeans are ripped and muddy, and they gape around in startled amazement. Each wears a lumpy, handspun wool sweater. They start to pull themselves together and get to their feet.

Dad makes an indistinct noise and hurries from the room. I turn to follow him, grabbing my backpack from Dad's chair on the way. In response to Mr. Willson's startled protest, I say, "My brothers are outside." He rushes to the window as I sprint out the door.

The boys are on their feet by the time I get outside. They're hugging each other and Dad, but they make room for me as soon as they see me.

"Well done, Em," Michael says as he pulls me in for a hug.

"Thanks, kiddo," Owen says, ruffling my hair.

"I knew you could do it," Stephen says quietly. But when I go to hug him, I see something that makes my heart stop. His sweater is the unfinished one. And the arm that should have gone into that missing sleeve isn't an arm—it's a wing.

"Oh, Stephen, I'm so sorry." I don't mean to whisper, but my voice won't come. I wanted this moment to be a triumph over Evelyn, but it feels an awful lot like failure.

"It's not your fault," he says, hugging me with his human arm.

"But baseball," I say.

He shrugs.

Dad looks about to burst from all his emotions. "Will you tell me what's going on now?"

"Everything," I say. The five of us start walking toward home. I don't bother signing out at the office. I'm pretty sure Mr. Willson is still watching us from his window anyway.

"It all started with Evelyn," I say.

Dad is very quiet as the boys tell what happened when Evelyn turned them into geese. Then I tell about all my time on YouTube and getting wool from Jeremy and working my butt off to make the wonky sweaters the boys are still wearing. When I finish, there's a long silence.

Dad finally says, "But why didn't you tell me any of this?"

"Because if I did, I wouldn't be able to bring them back. They'd be stuck that way forever."

"Wait," Owen interjects. "You mean you were riding to see us all those weekends without telling Dad where you were going?"

"You went to see them? Where?" I'm a little worried Dad's head might explode.

"At the reservoir. Hanging out with the ducks and the other geese."

"We never would have let you keep coming if we thought Dad didn't know."

I shrug.

"Did Evelyn know?" Dad asks.

I shrug again. "Probably. I didn't tell her."

He shakes his head. "I knew you two weren't getting along, but I didn't realize it was *this* bad."

"Who would?" Stephen says. "What parent expects...any of this?" He gestures with his wing.

When we get home, Evelyn is gone. Car, clothes, books, everything. I'm relieved, and I think Dad might be too. "Well, that saves us a big fight," I hear him mutter.

We order pizza and keep talking until late at night. I'm used to being up late now, and it feels good to watch the boys stuff themselves with human food. (Halfway through the evening we have to order more pizza.) I give the boys back their wallets and return Stephen's phone. It's a little hard to part with it now, after having all the information I need at my fingertips, but it was never mine.

The next day Dad surprises me with a phone of my own. "You've proven you can handle it," he says.

I hug him tight. "I'm sorry I lied and hid things from you."

"You did what you had to," he says. "I'm proud of you."

We don't go to school for the rest of the week, and Dad stays home from work too. We all need time to catch up on sleep and remember how to feed ourselves again, Dad says, but I think we also need a mini family vacation after all the stress. The boys are quieter now, especially Stephen. I overhear him talking with Dad about getting the wing amputated. It would be easier for Stephen to have only one arm than an arm and a wing, but I still feel weird about it.

The sweaters have all been put away in drawers. No one suggests getting rid of them, but I know no one will ever wear them again.

After school on Friday, Jeremy knocks on the door. He awkwardly hands me a little gift bag. I open it, confused. A skein of actual yarn and another pair of knitting needles. "It's cotton," he says. "I thought you might be sick of wool."

"Yeah," I laugh. I'm sick of knitting, too, but I don't tell him that. I might try it again sometime when my brothers' lives don't depend on it.

"It's…an apology," he says. "I'm sorry I talked to Miss Ainsley about you. You just seemed to be alone all the time, and I was worried about you."

I shrug. "It all worked out."

"Is Stephen home?"

I let Jeremy in and show him up to Stephen's room. My brother is lying on his bed reading, or pretending to read. We startle him so much, though, that I think he wasn't really seeing the words on the page.

Jeremy drops into the desk chair and turns it enough so that he includes me in the conversation, even as I stand in the doorway.

"So, I was thinking…. Want to try out for soccer in the fall?"

Stephen looks up at him.

"All feet, no hands," Jeremy shrugs. "I'll practice with you this summer, if you want."

"I've never been big on soccer," Stephen says, but I can tell he's been thinking about it.

"What about tennis?" I suggest.

Jeremy grins at me. "Mountain biking?"

"Horseback riding?"

163

"Sky diving?"

Stephen rolls his eyes at both of us. "You two are full of *great* ideas." He makes a face at me. "Go away, Em."

I stick my tongue out at him and head back downstairs, grinning. My brothers are home, my stepmother is gone. I pull my new phone out of my pocket. I'm going to call Laci and see if she's forgiven me and wants to hang out this weekend.

The Newt Prince

"I'm not kissing *that!*" Princess Adriana cried, recoiling. Her attendants looked at each other in confusion and concern, unsure of what to do with the man holding the small orange newt. He was as alarmed and perplexed as any of them.

But perhaps I should start at the beginning. Because this newt was, in fact, a prince.

Prince John was kind, good, loyal, and just. He had been raised well by parents who loved him and who loved their people enough that they wanted him to be a good king when they were gone. When he was of an age to be married, he heard a rumor about a princess of a distant kingdom who was so beautiful the stars and moon gazed on her in wonder. He set off to find out if the rumors were true.

Her beauty had not been exaggerated, and Prince John instantly decided that he must marry her. Princess Adriana had no shortage of suitors or marriage proposals, and she had turned them all down, for who was good enough for her? But she wouldn't find a better match than Prince John—he would adore her forever and be good to her, and she would never want for anything. She accepted his proposal, and the two had only to wait until he had prepared the bridal suite.

Prince John's mother, though eager for him to marry, worried that Princess Adriana may cause him grief before long. She had more experience than her son with beautiful women and with princesses in general, and she feared that Adriana's extraordinary beauty concealed a vain, selfish, and discontented heart. Her son was too infatuated to listen to her cautions, so she came up with a plan to test the princess's love.

The queen's grandmother had been a fairy, and the queen had enough fairy blood herself to do a little magic now and then. When Prince John came to bid her farewell before journeying back to claim his bride, she performed a spell on him to change his form. She gently picked up the tiny orange newt that used to be her son and that now looked at her reproachfully.

"It's for the best," she assured him. "All your princess must do to pass the test is kiss you and change you back." She gave the newt prince to his best friend who had been preparing to travel with him, instructing him to take Prince John directly to Princess Adriana.

This friend, Lord Rupert, did as he was bid, and rode fast toward Princess Adriana's kingdom so that his prince wouldn't have to be an amphibian for long.

But his effort was to no avail. Princess Adriana flatly refused to kiss the newt. "I'll kiss him as often as he likes when he's a man again. There must be another way to remove the spell."

Everything a newt could want, including a crystal bowl of clear water to swim in, was placed in a gilded cage to keep the tiny prince safe from the larger palace pets. It was set on the window ledge in Lord Rupert's room, as Princess Adriana couldn't abide the slimy slapping and splashing. While the prince was getting settled in his temporary new home, she called together her court magicians and any known fairies. They pondered and debated; they tried counter-spells and potions. Nothing worked. The princess had her ladies-in-waiting kiss the newt prince, but he remained small, orange, and slimy. This went on for days and weeks. Word spread that the princess's betrothed was stuck in the form of a newt, and a reward was offered for anyone who could change him back.

Around this time, the daughter of one of the castle gardeners came to visit her father. She had heard the rumors of the newt prince. While walking in the gardens, she saw the golden cage in the window and went to take a closer look. She had never seen such a miserable looking creature. Everything about the poor newt drooped. The girl's heart was moved with pity.

"Excuse me, my lord," she called to Lord Rupert. "Is this Prince John?"

"It is," he replied sadly.

"Might I take him into the garden awhile? It must be awful to be caged, even if it's for his own safety. I know the gardens here are not as fine as those he's used to, but there's a lovely pond to swim in. I could bring him back in an hour or so."

Lord Rupert, having felt terribly sorry for his friend for some time, and seeing the beauty and sweetness of the gardener's daughter, agreed to this arrangement. She carried him carefully to the pond and set him on its brim. "Please, Your Highness, stay within my sight. They will have my head if anything happens to you." The newt disappeared into the water. She watched his tiny orange shape flit back and forth across the pool a few times, then settled herself against a tree. The newt's eyes glittered at her from behind a floating leaf. She pulled knitting from her pocket and began to work, glancing again at the prince. She couldn't help laughing at his look of surprise. "Did you not know that a knitter always has her work at hand?" The newt slipped beneath the water and reappeared under a leaf farther away. "Forgive me for laughing, Your Highness," she said. "I have never seen any creature wear such an expression." It was clear that she had meant no offense, but no prince likes being laughed at, especially one who is already in an undignified situation. He stayed within eyeshot, but he didn't come near her again until she called him to go back inside.

The gardener's daughter returned again the next afternoon. The prince didn't look nearly as depressed today. She mentioned this to Lord Rupert.

"He has been much happier since his exercise outside yesterday," he confirmed.

"I suppose everyone was too busy trying to change you back to worry about whether you were a happy newt," she murmured to the newt prince as she carried him into the gardens. He disappeared into the pond the moment she lowered him close enough to dive in. She laughed to see his delight, glad to bring him a little joy. She took out her knitting and sat down, catching the ball of wool as it fell out of her pocket and rolled toward the pond. Prince John climbed onto the bank to investigate, looking very small next to the ball of yarn.

"It looks different from that perspective, doesn't it, Your Highness?" The gardener's daughter replaced the wool in her pocket. The newt watched her begin knitting before returning to his laps. "I'm making a new pair of winter stockings for my grandmother," she told him. He paused, listening, so she told him more. "We used to live in your own kingdom when I was a child, but then Grandmother fell ill, and we moved here to live with her and help her. She's been healthy for years now, and she'll be the first to say she doesn't need help, but she likes having us. I think she just likes having someone to have supper with, and to talk with by the fire at the end of the day." She smiled wistfully as she knit a few stitches. "I think we all want someone for that, don't you?"

She didn't wait for him to answer; he was nosing around in the moss anyway. She started humming to herself, just a nothing tune at first, then an old ballad she'd forgotten she knew. She couldn't remember the words, nor did she know what made her recall the melody just then. But it had an odd effect on the prince. He stopped what he was doing, turning to look at her over his wet orange shoulder. As she hummed, he moved closer, climbing onto her skirts to perch in a damp patch on her knee, all the while listening intently. When she stopped singing, they stared at each other for a moment, then he scampered back to the water and she laughed and returned to her work.

He was more social after that, though, occasionally climbing onto her lap to check on the progress of her stocking or just coming near to watch. When it was time to go back, she held out her hand, and he surprised her by skittering up her arm and perching on her shoulder. She giggled and brought him back to his golden cage, allowing him to run all the way back down her arm and inside.

When the gardener's daughter came the next day, she found the newt prince climbing the bars of the cage. She laughed as she opened the latch and he immediately scurried up her arm and onto her shoulder.

"What is your name?" Lord Rupert asked her.

"Tess," she said.

"Well, Tess, he's been waiting for you," he said with a grin.

"I'm honored." She smiled.

The newt prince darted here and there in the pond, coming

over occasionally to check on the gardener's daughter. The third time he climbed up onto her lap, leaving a wet trail, Tess put her knitting back in her pocket and scooped him up. She lifted him on the palm of her hand until they were eye to eye. He looked at her somewhat dolefully. She gave him a sympathetic smile.

"I do feel terribly sorry for you, Your Highness," Tess said. "You probably don't remember, but you were kind to me once as a child. I know it won't do any good, since I'm only a gardener's daughter, but for your sake, I'll try." She kissed him on the nose.

There was an explosion, and the gardener's daughter tumbled over backward as a man took the place of the newt she'd been holding. They both scrambled to their knees away from the edge of the pond and stared at each other. Tess felt her face go pink; Prince John was quite handsome, even with his curly brown hair dripping into his eyes and his tunic clinging damply to him.

"How did you do that?" he asked breathlessly. "Thank you, I mean, but how—"

"I don't know," she said. "I didn't expect it to work. I just felt sorry for you, and I figured everyone else had tried... well, everyone except—" she gestured to the castle, "who doesn't seem to be the one for you." Her brain caught up then with what she was saying. She clapped her hand over her mouth. "Forgive me, Your Highness! I have no right to an opinion on something like this."

"Don't apologize, you have every right," he said. "I'm actually inclined to agree with you."

At that moment, Lord Rupert burst upon them with a shout of "John!" He pulled the prince to his feet and embraced him. Tess blushed even brighter and stood, trying to be invisible.

She didn't need to try hard; Lord Rupert had eyes only for his friend. After demanding explanations that he was too excited to let the prince give, he suddenly cried, "Princess Adriana! She's been asking for you! I was sent to find you. She'll be delighted!" He put his arm around Prince John's shoulders and led him back toward the castle.

Tess wasn't sure whether to stay or go, whether she'd be rewarded or punished for freeing the newt prince, or whether she'd simply be ignored, as seemed the case. So she wandered the gardens until it was time to go home for dinner. She didn't go back to the castle the next day, or the next. It was no harder to invent a reason to stay home with her grandmother than it had been to find one to go to the castle. No one thought to ask her about it, and if she was a little more distracted than usual, no one thought to ask her about that either. In all the talk about the prince being freed by the kiss of a common girl, it never occurred to anyone that Tess might have been involved.

Now that Prince John was human again, Princess Adriana was ready to immediately begin wedding preparations, but he was less sure. He put her off by saying that he'd been a newt for so long that he wanted to go home and see his parents before the wedding, particularly since his mother was the one who'd put the spell on him, and he had some questions that needed answers. She let him go reluctantly, complaining that it was unfair of him to leave so soon after they were reunited. He left Lord Rupert behind to arrange his affairs; he was gone immediately.

The queen was surprised and delighted to see her son again and listened raptly to his story. When he had told her everything, she asked to meet the girl who had kissed him. A message was dispatched to Lord Rupert to bring her, if she would come. Tess was startled to see Lord Rupert at the door of her cottage, though not more startled than her family, to whom she had told nothing, but she agreed to go with him.

When they arrived at the home of Prince John, Lord Rupert brought her directly to a small receiving chamber.

"You'd probably rather get cleaned up first," he said apologetically, "but they've asked to see you right away."

He opened the door for her to enter.

Prince John and his mother were sitting inside, speaking in low voices. When the door opened and they saw who it was, the prince jumped to his feet and rushed over to her. He bowed low and kissed her hand.

"I did not thank you properly for restoring me to my human form," he said. "I don't think there are words to express how grateful I am."

"It was my pleasure, Your Highness," she said, blushing.

"Please, tell me," he said, "have we met before? You said I was kind to you as a child. When?"

She laughed. "Just once, when I was very young. My father used to work in your gardens here. One day I accidentally wandered into your private garden. When you found me, I was so afraid that I had gotten myself and my father into trouble. But you asked me to play instead of reprimanding me."

"It *is* you!" the prince exclaimed. "You laughed at my expression of surprise, but I've only ever seen someone pull a ball of yarn from their pocket once before, when you got it out to make—"

"A spider's web to catch butterflies." She smiled. "I'd forgotten."

"And that song you hummed by the pond—you were singing it when I found you in my garden. I remember I hid and listened for a while. You were so pretty that I thought you were a fairy."

She blushed. "No, not a fairy, just an ordinary girl."

He shook his head. "Not ordinary at all. Sweet Tess, will you marry me? You'll be my not-really-a-fairy princess, and I'll be your not-really-a-newt prince."

She laughed. "I'm afraid you'll be more disappointed by reality than I will. But what of Princess Adriana?"

"She never loved me—my time as a newt showed me that. And now that I know what true love is, I know that I never really loved her either." He shrugged.

"And your mother? Will she approve?" Tess couldn't quite repress a fear that the queen would turn *her* into a newt this time because she wasn't good enough for him.

"Wholeheartedly," the queen said, coming over. "I never told my son the full requirements of the spell: it would only break with a kiss from his true love. I designed it to test Princess Adriana's heart. If she really loved you, John, she would kiss you even in such an unappealing form. If she refused, I expected Lord Rupert to bring you home to me and I would reverse the spell immediately."

"I was about to," Lord Rupert put in, "when this young lady came along. He seemed to enjoy his outings with her so much that I decided that delaying a few more days couldn't hurt."

"It certainly couldn't," Prince John said, smiling at Tess.

"Then the test for Princess Adriana ended up testing me as well?" she asked.

The queen nodded, smiling. "You passed beautifully, dear."

"You still haven't answered my question," the prince said, taking both of Tess's hands in his. "You've held a portion of my heart since that day when we were children, and I believe you're the only one who could ever hold the whole thing. Will you marry me?"

"I will," she said.

He took her in his arms and kissed her. It was much nicer, and less wet, than when she'd kissed him the first time. They were married the very next day.

Lord Rupert was sent to get Tess's father and grandmother and bring them back to live in the palace. Her father had missed the gardens that he had tended for many years and was glad to see them again, but he could not enjoy them unless he had his hands dirty as well. He was given the care of the prince and princess's private garden, and it was the most splendid garden of all.

Photo © Megan Angstadt-Williams

Bonus: Goose Brothers Sweater Pattern

Pattern Notes: This sweater is designed to be worn with 4-6 inches (10-15 cm) of positive ease. Follow the instructions for the size that is that amount larger than your actual bust/chest size.

The body of this sweater is constructed of two rectangles for the front and back. The sleeves are shaped with simple increase stitches for more comfort and wearability. If you'd prefer to make it exactly as Emma did in the story "Goose Brothers," with no shaping, follow the *Emma Variant* instructions in the pattern.

Needle: US size 9 (5.5mm), or size needed to obtain gauge.
Yarn Used: Lion Brand Feels Like Butta Yarn (weight 4; 100% polyester; 590 yards/275g) in Sage.
Approximate Yardage: 340 (510, 803, 900, 980, 1065, 1172, 1281, 1366, 1502) yards.
Gauge (Unblocked): 18 stitches and 27 rows in 4 inches.

Other Notions: yarn needle for finishing.

Final Measurements:

Pattern is written 3XS (2XS, XS, S, M, L, XL, 2XL, 3XL, 4XL).
Bust: 26 (30, 34, 38, 42, 46, 50, 54, 58, 62) inches or 66 (76, 86, 96.5, 107, 117, 127, 137, 147, 157.5) cm.
Length (shoulder to hem): 13 (17, 24, 25, 25, 25, 26, 26, 26, 27) inches or 33 (43, 61, 63, 63, 63, 66, 66, 66, 69) cm.

Stitch Abbreviations:

k = knit

p = purl

k1fb = knit one in front and back. Knit stitch through front loop, do not slide off left needle. Knit same stitch through back loop, then slide off left needle (1 stitch increased).

Pattern:

Body (Make 2):

Cast on 59 (68, 77, 86, 95, 104, 113, 122, 131, 140) stitches.
First 14 rows: knit.
Row 15: knit.
Row 16: purl.
Repeat Rows 15 and 16 until piece measures 12 (16, 23, 24, 24, 24, 25, 25, 25, 26) inches or 30 (40.5, 58, 61, 61, 61, 63, 63, 63, 66) cm from cast on edge.
Next 8 rows: knit.
Bind off.

Emma Variant: Cast on 59 (68, 77, 86, 95, 104, 113, 122, 131, 140) stitches. Knit all rows until piece measures 13 (17, 24, 25, 25, 25, 26, 26, 26, 27) inches or 32.5 (43, 60.5, 63.5, 63.5, 63.5, 65.5, 65.5, 65.5, 68.5) cm from cast on edge. Bind off.

Sleeve (Make 2):

Cast on 31 (32, 36, 36, 36, 40, 40, 41, 45, 45) stitches.
First 8 rows: knit.
Row 9: k1, k1fb, k to last 2 sts, k1fb, k1.
Row 10: purl.
Row 11: knit.
Row 12: purl.
Repeat Rows 11 and 12 another 2 (2, 3, 2, 2, 2, 1, 0, 0, 0) times.
Repeat Rows 9-12 (plus repeats) a total of 8 (10, 11, 12, 14, 14, 17, 21, 23, 26) times until you have 47 (52, 58, 60, 64, 68, 74, 83, 91, 97) stitches.
Repeat Rows 11 and 12 another 5 (5, 2, 9, 1, 1, 2, 11, 6, 0) times.
Bind off.

Emma Variant: Cast on 47 (52, 58, 60, 64, 68, 74, 83, 91, 97) stitches. Knit all rows until piece measures 12 (14.5, 18, 18, 18, 18, 17, 17, 16.5, 16.5) inches or 29 (35, 46, 46, 46, 46, 43, 43, 42, 42) cm from cast on edge.

Sew Shoulders:
Hold front and back body pieces together so that bind off edges line up. Sew 3.5 (4, 4.5, 5, 6, 6.5, 7, 7.5, 8.5, 9) inches or 9 (10, 11.5, 13, 15, 16.5, 18, 19, 21.5, 23) cm from each side, leaving center neck open. This seam is the center of the shoulder. (*Figure 1*)

Sew sleeve bind off edge to sides of front and back at shoulder, matching center of sleeve edge with shoulder seam. (*Figure 2*)

Sew Sides:

Lay flat so that front and back are wrong sides together, and so that sleeves are folded in half lengthwise. Sew up sides of front and back and down sleeves. (*Figure 3*)

Sew all ends under.

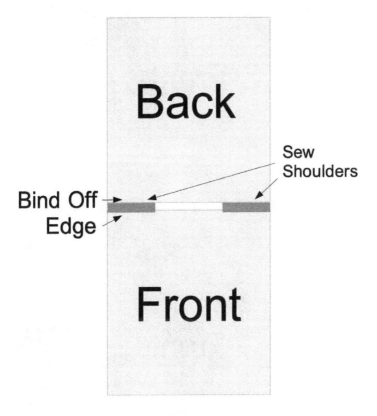

Figure 1

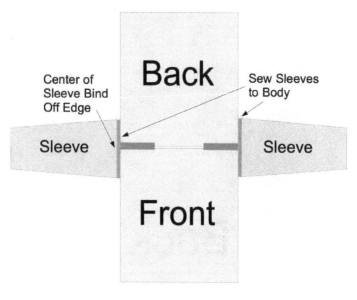

Figure 2

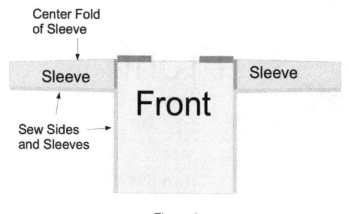

Figure 3

Glossary

Carding: the process by which fibers (of wool, cotton, flax, etc.) are separated and prepared for spinning.

Crochet: a handicraft in which yarn is turned into fabric using a small hook.

Double-Pointed Needles: a set of (usually four) knitting needles with a point on either end, used for knitting small items in the round, like socks, mittens, or fairy-sized sweaters.

Gauge: a measurement of how big knit or crochet stitches are, usually measured in stitches per inch/cm and rows per inch/cm.

Hank: a coiled or wrapped unit of yarn, often twisted and twisted back on itself.

Knitting: a handicraft in which yarn is turned into fabric using two long needles.

Loom: a machine used to weave fabric from yarn or thread.

Mordant: a substance used in dyeing fabric or wool that fixes or sets the dye so that it doesn't fade.

Raglan: a type of sweater with sleeves that extend to the collar without shoulder seams. These are often knit from the top down.

Rolag: a small roll of fiber, prepared for spinning using hand-carders.

Roving: a long, narrow bundle of fiber for spinning.

Shuttle: a device used with a loom to carry the weft threads (the ones that go across, side to side) back and forth during weaving.

Treadle(s): the foot pedal(s) used to control the motion of a spinning wheel or loom.

Warp: the vertical threads on a loom, which are placed first. The weft threads (side to side) are woven through these warp (up and down) threads.

Acknowledgements

I'd like to thank everyone who has supported me and helped me in publishing this book and in my overall writing life:

My parents, who have always supported me, and my husband, the calm voice of reason who never doubted that I could do this.

Becki, my biggest cheerleader.

Megan, for her friendship and gorgeous photos.

Melanie (@threadbender), for letting me—a complete stranger but fellow yarn lover—use a photo of her beautiful hand-spun wool on the cover.

My editor, Lucia Ferrara, for invaluable advice and wisdom.

My critique group, for encouraging me.

Hans Christian Andersen, for writing "The Wild Swans," which is one of my favorite fairy tales and the basis for "Goose Brothers." And to everyone else who's ever written a fairy tale, because I've been influenced by so many.

And most importantly, I'd like to thank God, my heavenly Father, for creating this nerd and loving me just as I am.

Thank you all. I couldn't have done this without you.

Sign up for Eliza's newsletter at elizaprokopovits.com/email for new release updates and more.